Home to Derry

Home to Derry

Tomás Ó Canainn

Appletree Press

First published in 1986 by

Appletree Press Ltd
The Old Potato Station
14 Howard Street South
Belfast BT7 1AP
Tel: +44 (0) 28 9024 3074
Fax: +44 (0) 28 9024 6756
E-mail: reception@appletree.ie
Web Site: www.irelandseye.com

Editor: Jean Brown
Designer: Stuart Wilkinson
Production Manager: Paul McAvoy

Home to Derry

ISBN: 0 86281 932 6

9 8 7 6 5 4 3 2 1

AP3201

To Brid,
- the gentle galvaniser

Chapter One

It was half past seven on a fresh spring morning – time for himself and Jenny to go out on the streets, collecting horse-dung. Their mother had been brought up on a farm near Dungiven and was a firm believer in the magic power exercised by horse-dung on potatoes and rhubarb. Apart from a few lupins and dahlias, those were the only crops that grew in the tiny back garden of their house in Barry Street. High walls kept the sun away from all but the tops of the thrusting lupins, even in highest summer. Sean stood at the kitchen door and looked at the little yard between himself and the garden, which was closed in on two sides by the white-washed walls of their own house and, on the third, by the side gable of Mrs Park's house.

'For God's sake take that bucket and shovel and get out of my sight this minute.'

Sean's mother had finally lost her patience with them and he knew well, even if his young sister Jenny did not seem to, that there was no longer any option.

'I'm sick, sore and tired of lookin' at the pair of you. The quicker you get started the quicker it'll be over and I'll have breakfast ready when youse come back. I'm goin' up now to rise Brid and the weans.'

His mother turned away from the scullery door, crossed the kitchen, where her newly-lit fire was crackling in the iron range, and went into the hall. He heard the quick creaking of the stairs as she went up. Her voice came back to him urgently: 'Give that porridge a stir before you go.' She thought of everything. A widow with five young children probably had to.

He wondered why he and Jenny always got the dirty job of collecting the dung. It needed two people alright, for it had to be done quickly and unobtrusively, lest any of the neighbours might see you. That would be the final indignity. He had to admit that the so-called weans – his younger brother Eamonn and Mary, the baby of the family – were too young for the job, while his elder sister Brid did more than her share of the housework. Still, he wished it could be anybody but himself who was out there shovelling shit before breakfast.

'Are youse not away yet?'

His mother's voice came at him from the kitchen. Through the window he could see the weans up beside the fire, shivering and sleepy. Brid was pulling a jumper down over young Mary's head and the long curls tangled in a button. The child screamed and was suddenly wide awake.

'Here, show us that,' said the mother, easing the button out of the long strands of hair. 'I'll give it a rub and you'll be as right as rain in no time.'

She caressed the child's head and turned to Brid. 'Get Eamonn's shoes on him and lace them up.'

Jenny decided it was time to make her last stand against the horse-dung excursion.

'I'm just not goin' out there. I don't care what anybody says – I'm not for goin'.'

She puffed out her cheeks and held her breath till she was red in the face. It was a pose they all recognised and since she always adopted it whenever anyone wanted to take her photograph, it was recorded on every single family portrait in their possession. Photographs were things Jenny did not agree with and her famous 'puss', as the family called it, was her gesture of non-cooperation.

'Would you listen to her,' his mother said. 'You'd think the whole of Derry city was goin' to be out there lookin' at youse, the way you're goin' on about it. You'll be the sorry pair if I have to rise to you again.'

Sean could see his mother's face through the window and he knew she meant business this time. Her lips tightened and a muscle moved in the side of her face. He didn't particularly want to feel the strap stinging his bare legs, but Jenny just stood here, daring her mother to act.

The confrontation was short-lived: his mother moved quickly, bundling Jenny, bucket and shovel out the back door.

'Go on outa that, you big hallion,' she shouted, slamming the door and shooting the bolt home with finality.

He thought Jenny was relieved to have escaped so easily but she didn't say anything as they walked up the back lane together. He stayed on the right, beside the Barry Street backdoors, while she kept to the other side, near the backdoors of Meadowbank Avenue. Between them was the dried-up bed of the streamlet which meandered down the lane on rainy days. At the top of the lane they turned left towards Meadowbank: they would not have dreamed of looking for dung in Barry Street, where they might be recognised by the neighbours. Meadowbank was a higher class street, right enough, but it had two advantages – not so many people knew them there and it was a much steeper street, particularly above the junction with Richmond Crescent, and you'd often find that the milkman's pony might have felt the need to relieve himself on the way up or down.

They were in luck today. The steam was still rising from a newly-deposited prize, right in the middle of the road. Jenny ran forward with the bucket.

'Put it down there,' said Sean, 'and keep nix at the corner. Give us a shout if you see anybody comin'.'

He had become pretty adept at flicking the dung on to the shovel and straight into the bucket. He glanced quickly down the street. Miss Mooney's cat walked along the low garden wall and eyed him curiously. The cooing of pigeons up at Douglas's corner was the only sound. The dung smelt strong and sickening. He knew it had not come from the milkman's puny animal, which would have been incapable of matching this product for quality or size. His mother would be pleased: there was no doubt in his mind about that.

'Hurry up,' said Jenny, 'there's a man from Governor Road comin' over the top lane.'

In his hurry he let the dung fall from the shovel. He jumped with fright as a boat on the Foyle blew its horn. The sound jarred the quiet of the street.

'Where is he now, Jenny?'

'It's alright, he's away down Barry Street: have you not it done yet?'

'Come over here quick and give us a hand.'

She ran over to him and he handed her the stick: 'Push it on to the shovel,' he whispered urgently.

She held her nose, half-closed her eyes and did as she was told.

'Ugh, what a stink.' The words squeezed out through her clenched teeth.

'Come on, keep at it,' he urged, 'we're nearly there.'

They heard the clip-clop of horse's hooves from Duncreggan Road and the constant crunch of cartwheels on the tarmacadam. There was no mistaking the milk-cart, even at this distance, and you could hear the clanging of the small can which hung from the brass tap on the big creamery can and swung furiously to and fro as the pony trotted.

Even as he listened it became obvious to him that the animal which had passed this way earlier must have been one of the big dray horses, pulling heavy loads from the docks. That would explain everything: sorting out the problem satisfactorily in his mind made him feel good, but the most important thing of all was that it meant a half-bucketful of dung for his mother. Maybe the milk-horse would do them a similar favour now.

They hid bucket, shovel and stick around the corner in the back lane of the Richmond Crescent houses and stood hopefully watching the pony as it approached them. The milkman pulled at his pipe, flicked the reins and nodded to them as he passed. But they were concentrating on the pony. Half-way down Meadowbank it lifted its tail and it seemed that God was on their side.

'Look at that – look!' Jenny caught his arm in her excitement. It was only a false alarm, though, and their dreams of a nearly full bucket vanished with the dropping tail. They did not need to walk on down Meadowbank to know that it was dungless. One acquired a certain skill in these matters, and spotting material from fifty yards was no problem.

'Let's go over to the far field where the donkey is.'

Sean led the way across Richmond Crescent. There were houses on one side only and the 'near-field' lay on their left. He was glad they were both wearing sandals, which made no noise on the pavement. This was dangerous territory. Most of his friends lived in the Crescent: while the drawn blinds meant that they were probably still in bed, one could never be absolutely certain of not being spied upon. A number of them were the sons of RUC men and the Law always liked to know who was doing what and where and when and why.

The sad-looking donkey was tethered to a stake by a long rope. Sean could see the mark of the cross on his back and thought of the story he had learned at school about all donkeys bearing the same dark-brown cross on their backs as a mark of special favour, for having carried Our Lord triumphantly into Jerusalem. Jenny thought it was because a donkey had carried Mary to Bethlehem just before Jesus was born. Wasn't there a donkey involved in the Flight into Egypt as well? He seemed to remember a picture of it somewhere. There was another donkey-image troubling him and he tried to put it out of his mind. There was nothing biblical about it: it concerned this very donkey in front of them. The animal regularly demonstrated a monster of an erection, which was entirely at odds with the docile image of the carrier of the Saviour of the world.

They had been playing football the first day the phenomenon made its appearance from the donkey's belly. The game was forgotten as they watched, fascinated, but filled with guilt. The unholy size of it was completely unexpected on that first showing. It was not so breath-taking an experience after that, when it began to happen regularly, but Sean couldn't help watching, even though it confused him more than a little.

But there was a practical job to be done now and plenty of dung in the vicinity. That was the great advantage of tethering, though the poor donkey probably did not appreciate that. Sean began to fill the bucket.

'It's not the same,' said Jenny, looking critically at what he had collected. 'Mum won't take that stuff – she said horse-manure and that's what she meant.'

But the bucket was nearly full now and it was easy stuff to shovel-up from the grass.

'Come on, Jenny, let's go.'

They started back towards the Crescent, carrying the bucket between them. Only another five minutes and they'd be safely home. They could see Sergeant Clements wheeling his bicycle out the front gate of his house: it must be later than they had thought, if he was going on duty already. His bicycle was one of those big 'bedsteads', for he was a heavy man. Sean could almost feel the shock to the bicycle's system as that fourteen stone of law-abiding body came relentlessly down on it. They hid the bucket in the grass and stood in front of it, waiting for him to pass.

'We can't go back the way we came,' said Sean. 'It's too late now: we'll be seen.'

They decided on the detour down by Catherwood's bus-garage and along the Strand Road, passing the full length of Bryce and Weston's shirt factory. It meant that they avoided the Crescent and most of Meadowbank Avenue. Even though the Strand Road, which was a main thoroughfare, would be getting busy by this time, going that way was infinitely preferable to taking the risk of someone peeping at them from behind a bedroom curtain in Richmond Crescent. They raced all the way along the Strand, the bucket swinging awkwardly between them, and went up Meadowbank as far as the bottom lane. Only once were they in danger of being spotted, when Mr Douglas, who drove the street-cleaning lorry, came down Meadowbank with circular brushes whirring. The factory door was their refuge, before the final fifty-yard dash up the lane and in the back gate, slamming it gratefully behind them.

'That's my last time ever: I don't care what anybody says,' panted Jenny, when she got her breath back.

She watched her brother taking the bucket into the middle of the tiny garden. She herself was so winded that she had to stay leaning against the back gate. Before anyone from the house had a chance to come out and inspect the contents of the bucket, Sean had up-ended it on the garden so that, as far as the untrained eye could see, a goodly pile of fresh horse-dung had just been delivered. The secret of the donkey-dung was safe.

Chapter Two

Sean and Brid sat on the stairs, waiting for the postman. It was a fine place to sit and enjoy the soft comfort of carpet under you: the only other part of the house with that sort of luxury was the parlour, but they only went in there on Sundays, or when very special visitors arrived.

Sean could see through the coloured glass panels in the vestibule door, because the double front door was open to let in the light. It cast a lovely pattern of green and red on the tiled floor of the hall and continued on to the hallstand. Only the family's best coats hung there: ordinary coats were kept under the stairs and you entered the dark den through a little door in the scullery.

Brid and himself had kept their postman's vigil these last three mornings, hoping to be the first in the house to get Mrs McAloon's answer to their mother's letter. It was a full week since his mother had written to Mrs McAloon, who owned a boarding-house in Portstewart. The strain of not knowing whether she could take the family for its annual holiday or not was becoming unbearable.

The hall darkened as the postman's bulk shut off the light from the vestibule door. Brid was on her feet before Sean realised what was happening, but he caught her as she put her hand on the door-handle.

'Mammy, he took the letter, after me bein' there first. Tell him to give it back to me at once.'

It was too late and Sean was already reading the envelope: 'Mrs Bridie Kane, 9 Barry Street, Derry.'

'Let me read the postmark,' Brid appealed to her mother. 'Mammy, tell him to let me read the postmark.'

His mother took the letter sharply from his hand, but not before he had got a clear picture of the stamp and the printed writing beside it.

Brid turned the letter sideways in her hand, trying to decipher the smudged postmark. 'P-O-R-T-S-T-E... Portstewart, Co. Derry. It's from Mrs McAloon, Mammy: will I open it?'

'Give it to Mammy,' Jenny interrupted, 'Sure you can't read big people's writing.'

'I can so – can't I Mammy?' Brid needed the reassurance and got it from her mother, but she was glad enough to hand over the short note from Mrs McAloon.

'Dear Bridie,' her mother read aloud, but then lapsed into silence: only her lips moved as she concentrated on Mrs McAloon's handwriting.

As she continued to read it to herself, Jenny spoke out for them all: 'What does she say?'

'Shh!' Her mother quietened her without looking up, folded the letter, put it into the envelope and slipped it in behind the clock on the mantelpiece. Only then did she break her silence.

'She'll have our room ready by teatime on Monday.'

Jenny turned to Eamonn and Mary: 'We're goin' to Portstewart on wur holidays.' Her face was bright with the excitement of it all.

'Are we goin' as well?' Sean felt a bit sorry that Eamonn had to put the question. The weans couldn't assume they were included in the plan, since they were so often excluded from pleasure trips to town or even to the shops at the bottom of the street. It was always either too late or too early, too dark or too cold for the weans to be let out with the older three children.

'Of course you're goin'. We're all off on wur holidays to the Port,' said Sean. 'An' we'll get sweets an' ice-cream every day a' we can sail my wee boat in the swimming-pool an' fish off the rocks an' everything.'

His mother interrupted Sean's dream with harsh reality: 'There'll be no goin' anywhere till this house is red up and shinin' like a new pin. You take that wee brush, Sean, and do the stairs. Jenny can scrub the front step and the weans can do the dishes, for I have to finish them skirts for Brid and Jenny, not to mention that heap of darnin' over there. Brid, you can black-lead the range, but put an apron on you!'

If there was one job Sean did not like, it was brushing down the stairs. His mother insisted on brisk strokes with the stiff hand-brush and you'd feel the dust in your mouth and nose and see it on the backs of your hands. Even after all that you'd still have to go back with a duster to clean and polish the painted wood on both sides of the narrow stair-carpet. You couldn't cut corners on the job either, for she'd be there to inspect it before there was any question of being allowed out to play. But it was all worthwhile if it meant getting to Portstewart on Monday.

The long Friday finished at last and a lazy Saturday dragged itself towards Sunday.

The whole Kane family was seated in a row in the seventh seat from the front of the church. They always sat there, with Mrs Kane at the end to make sure that none of them could stray on to the aisle.

Sean thought he was a bit too old for a white sailor's suit – a present from his Uncle Joe in America. It had come in a parcel full of dresses for the girls. Brid was wearing one of them now, all red and frilly and not the sort of thing you would get in the Derry shops. She was the serious one of the family, and performed the same containing function at the other end of the family group as her mother did at the aisle.

'Mammy said to kneel up straight and say your prayers.' It was Jenny who gave him the message: he knew it was genuine, as his mother was looking sternly in his direction and indicating that he should straighten up. He pulled himself forward unwillingly, regretting the absence of support from the seat. His mother sometimes judged Catholics by how they knelt in church and actively discouraged lapses in her own family. He opened the prayer-book again and tried to read the Memorare: 'Remember O most gracious Virgin Mary that never was it known that anyone who fled to thy protection, implored thy aid or sought thy intercession was left unaided by thee…'

The prayer-book had been his father's and contained a prayer for seamen, as well as a prayer for the King. He thought a king shouldn't need his prayers, but you couldn't be sure. He turned the page and saw the picture of the crucifix… 'Behold O kind and most sweet Jesus, I cast myself upon my knees in thy sight…' He liked the 'En Ego': it was more valuable than some of the other prayers which merited a mere three hundred days indulgence. A plenary indulgence was always worth having, but you had to do everything just right to qualify: they said at school that one Our Father, one Hail Mary and one Gloria after it would do the job, but his mother insisted that it had to be six of each, which was not so easy.

He wondered about the thirty days prayer: it might solve his problem. He scanned the conditions: '…by the devout recital of which, for the above space of time, we may hope to obtain any lawful request.' The word 'lawful' was the snag. Would God think that his prayers for Sue Mackey's conversion were lawful? Praying for a red-haired Protestant girl with freckles to become a Catholic so that she could marry him didn't seem quite right, particularly when she appeared happy enough in her Protestant state. A terrible thought came into his mind: why shouldn't he become a Protestant and marry her? It would certainly be a more practical solution. Protestants seemed to get on a lot better than Catholics in Derry. He was shocked at his own daring in toying with such thoughts. He looked guiltily across at his mother, in case she had somehow divined what was in his head. But it was nice to be thinking of Sue Mackey: the way she ran – as fast as any of the lads – or her speed off the mark in rounders. They said she was good at school, too: he liked that about her.

The thirty days prayer was all of five pages long and didn't offer any indulgences. Sean took that as a good sign of its efficacy: it seemed to be just a straight contract between God and himself, with the Blessed Virgin Mary as a go-between. He had never tried a five-page prayer before, but then he had never in all his life wanted anything with the same intensity that he wanted this: He'd start tomorrow in Portstewart.

Fr O'Loughlin was reading out the stipends now: everybody was listening carefully – far more carefully than they listened to his sermon. He was a soft-spoken man and owned a big St Bernard dog which had knocked Sean down one day as he passed.

'Mrs B. Kane, 9 Barry Street, two shilling and sixpence.' It was a bit above average for Barry Street and sixpence more than last year, though his mother couldn't really afford it. The Culmore Road people who headed the list always gave a pound, but they were in a different world.

'Mr and Mrs J. McCarron, 13 Barry Street, one shilling.' They had more money than his mother, but seemed to have no great interest in advancing themselves. Some people were like that.

He'd have to go across the Crescent later, to see if there was any chance of saying hello to Sue as she came back from Sunday school. He'd call for Ger McCabe first and it wouldn't be so obvious if the two of them just happened to be chatting together near Mackey's door. Ger would come with him – no doubt about that: he was mad about Sue's young sister Babs.

Fr O'Loughlin turned to give the final blessing and the end of the mass was in sight at last. Sean's mind was made up now about the thirty days prayer. He did a perfect genuflection under the watchful eye of his mother and followed Jenny down the aisle and out into the bright sunlight. It was going to be a great day.

Ger and himself spent a long time that afternoon outside the Mackey's front gate. The Crescent was quiet, for Protestants didn't play games on Sundays and many Catholics considered that was a good example to follow. Peter Bentham, accompanied by his mother and father, passed them with scarcely a nod. This was no surprise, even though Peter was their friend and played with them every day: Prods were different on a Sunday and you'd get used to that. The good suit and the peaked cap pulled down over the eyes and the big Bible under the arm were declarations of that difference.

'I don't think they're in the house at all,' Ger said impatiently. 'Come on round their back lane and peep over the wall.'

Richmond Crescent houses had been built into the slope of the hill, looking down towards the factory and the Strand Road: beyond that was the Lough Swilly railway station, separated from the river Foyle by the shipyard. The high back lane of the Crescent meant that one could see over the wall at the bottom of Mackey's sloping garden, right into the kitchen. It was a simple matter for an adult to glance in as he passed along the lane, but it was much more difficult for children, who did not have the necessary height.

Sean gave a little leap in the air as he passed and tried to see as much as he could of the Mackey's kitchen in the fraction of a second that he was airborne. Ger was smaller, but a better jumper, so they both had about the same short time to ascertain if their true loves were at home. Even if they were, there was no hope of actually talking to them on a Sunday, but even a distant glance of a half-second's duration was worth risking a lot for. Both lads knew that they had to be subtle about it too, as if they were casually walking by and giving two equally casual leaps in the air. One wouldn't like anyone to get suspicious, least of all Mr Mackey, who was in the RUC.

But a half-second look was not enough to let one's eyes get accustomed to the indistinct view through the window. They continued their walk right along the back lane, turned round into the front of the Crescent and completed the circle by aiming for the back lane again: it was all low-key and casual, so that no-one would be any the wiser. Another pair of jumps at the back of Mackey's let them know that there was definitely someone at home, but they had to do the full round of the Crescent again before they could venture another look. As they performed their next despairing leaps, completely disregarding subtlety so as to get a longer view of the kitchen, they were left in no doubt that someone was there: they recognised their true loves' father, making unmistakeable signals to them to be off – and quick about it! They ran.

Chapter Three

Five of them struggled to close the suitcase on Monday morning. It was a big old-fashioned expanding one which normally lay under his mother's bed and still carried the old labels with their Coleraine and Glasgow addresses. The four children sat on it and ever so gradually the two halves of the lock came nearer and nearer together. His mother encouraged them in their efforts, but Jenny saw the funny side of it. 'We can't get any heavier, Mammy, no matter what you say.'

Sean had enjoyed the packing: he had managed to slip in the playing cards when his mother wasn't looking, as well as the small wooden boat Uncle Manny had made for him. Eamonn's fishing rod had been refused entry: it was of his own design and manufacture and looked it. He was still determined to bring it with him.

'Push hard,' his mother urged. 'All together now.'

Sean was seated nearest the stubborn lock. He jumped up and landed again with a thud. The lock clicked into place and the job was done.

Their next-door neighbour, Mr Smith, came in to see them off and carried the case down to the bus-stop on the Strand Road, as they had to travel by bus to the Waterside to get the LMS train.

When the bus arrived the conductor looked doubtfully at the

enormous case. 'Are youse emigratin' or what?'

Nobody got out of the bus, as Barry Street was only a couple of stops from the terminus on the Buncrana Road.

'Hurry up there,' shouted the conductor. 'I'll do the furniture-removing when you're in.'

Even though there was plenty of room on the bus they all crowded into two seats. His mother and the two weans were in one and Sean, Brid and Jenny in the other: this arrangement often inspired sympathetic conductors to be lenient about the fares.

'One and three halves to the LMS.' His mother tried to sound confident.

'There's five there,' the conductor said. He was probably still thinking of the weight of the suitcase.

'Surely be to God you're not chargin' us for them wee weans?'

He capitulated ungraciously in the face of such psychological pressure.

Most of the shoppers got out at Great James's Street, which was at the town end of the Strand Road, and others descended at Guildhall Square. These last made their way under the Walls of Derry at Shipquay Gate and ascended the steep slope of Shipquay Street towards the Diamond. It was there the hiring fairs used to be held and the servant boys and girls from Donegal lined up to be viewed by the Derry farmers. Sean's mother often talked about such things when they'd all be gathered in the kitchen at night. Knitting socks seemed to induce that sort of mood in her: it was as if she wanted to keep renewing the memories in her own mind. Even the thought of his mother's storytelling made him feel warm and comforted. She was a different mother when she told her stories.

The Guildhall clock boomed out the hour and the bus moved off again after the long stop. It rattled on the rough cobblestones of narrow Foyle Street before emerging into the bright width of John Street. The seagulls dipped and rose beside the Glasgow boat as the bus crossed Craigavon Bridge. When they turned left into Duke Street the way was blocked by a herd of steamy, tired cattle coming in from the country. A man and two young fellows beat them with sticks to try and clear a way for the bus. The driver edged his way through and Sean could feel and hear the thud of the animals' weight against the sides of the bus. They reached the station at last and only then did Sean accept the reality of his impending seaside holiday.

Steam was everywhere in the station and the smell of smoke. On the footplate of the engine a sweating, black-faced fireman shovelled endless coat into the hot blaze, while the driver checked his gauges and cleaned the various wheels and levers with a rag, well satisfied with himself. Down between the carriages another railwayman with a crowbar lifted the heaviest iron chain Sean had ever seen and dropped it over an enormous hook to hold the two carriages together. The station-master blew his whistle sharply and they panicked. The guard held open the door of an empty carriage and they gathered themselves into it, happy that they'd be alone, at least until the first stop at Ballykelly or Limavady Junction. Another whistle – the real thing this time – and the wave of a green flag as the first long and powerful exhaust of steam from the cylinders of the engine moved them off smoothly. Sean could see the guard running to jump into his own carriage, banging the door after him. The engine seemed to rest momentarily after its initial big effort and the carriages lurched together. By the time all the jerking was done and the train moving sweetly as a unit, they were out of the station and leaving Derry behind. Across the expanse of Lough Foyle he could see the whole city. It was easy to find Barry Street, as the Factory was clearly visible and Pennyburn Church as well. He had no view of the Crescent, hidden behind the Factory, but he thought he could just make out the top of Meadowbank, before the train turned around the bend of the Lough and pointed its nose to Coleraine.

They had been travelling for half an hour when the girls screamed as they were all plunged unexpectedly into the blackness of a tunnel and smoke poured in through the open window.

'Shut the window, Sean – quick.'

He pulled at the strap but could not free it. His mother leaned across – he could feel her hand in the darkness as she jerked the strap forward to free it from its stud: together they pulled it down and heard the window clicking shut. All was suddenly quieter inside the carriage.

He tried to frighten Jenny and the weans with talk of the bogey-man, but didn't have much success, at least with Jenny, until his fingers moving lightly on her neck convinced her that a spider had landed in the awful darkness. She gave a piercing scream just as they emerged into the light. It was only a momentary break, before the train was swallowed up again in the blackness of the second tunnel.

They were just beginning to enjoy it all when the seaside brightness of Downhill presented itself at the window. The sun explored every facet of the sparkling waves as they came rolling up the beach and ran back down like molten silver. Through the other window Sean could see the rush of the tumbling waterfall and his eyes followed its path to the sea. It streamed out from the bottom of the cliff, ran beneath the railway line and emerged at the top of the strand in a spreading series of rivulets.

The sand dunes of Portstewart seemed very near as the train turned at the mouth of the river Bann to follow its course to Coleraine. They would then have to change to a smaller train and make their way back along the other side of the river to Portstewart. Mrs Kane started to busy herself with preparations for the changeover and the children pulled on coats and gathered their small belongings. As the train entered the station she bent to look out of the window, hoping to see Hugh Stinson on the platform.

Hugh was assistant station-master and he had been their next-door neighbour when they lived in Windsor Avenue in Coleraine, until the death of her husband, Eamonn Kane. She never tired of telling the children what a wonderful man Hugh was: meeting him on the Coleraine station platform was something she looked forward to every year.

'Hugh – Mr Stinson,' she called out to him as the train squealed to a halt. Eamonn was thrown against her and the big hook on his fishing rod, all ready for the Portstewart fish, caught his mother instead. No amount of jiggling could free it: the more they tried the more firmly the barb embedded itself into the back of her best coat.

'All change for Portrush and Portstewart,' the guard shouted at them.

'Quick now, or it's Belfast you'll be spending your holidays in.'

Hugh Stinson lifted out the big case and left it on a trolley beside them.

'Just hold on for a wee minute, Bridie, till we get the Belfast train out and I'll see you across the bridge to the Portstewart train.'

'But is she not ready to go immediately? We might miss her.'

'Divil the fear o' that,' said Hugh. 'She won't budge till I give the signal.'

All this time Eamonn stood behind his mother with the fishing rod in his hand. He had let out some of the line so that he could walk discreetly behind her, a few yards distant, in the hope that his 'catch' would not be too obvious.

His mother was still distressed by it: 'I'm never going to live down this disgrace.' She turned to Eamonn: 'Just wait till I get you home.'

Sean and Jenny thought that a great joke, since they weren't going home, but Eamonn took his mother's threat seriously.

He let out some more line to distance himself from her.

'They'll think you caught a whale, Eamonn.' Jenny laughed as she spoke.

They crossed over the bridge and were enveloped in smoke and steam from the departing Belfast train. The whole station shook beneath their feet as the engine powered its way out of the station. A bell clanged and the level-crossing gates opened for their train. Hugh Stinson took his time in helping them into a carriage and warned the guard to give them special attention. Only then did he wave his flag. The whistle blew and they were on the last lap.

Portstewart was the Catholic seaside resort and nearby Portrush the Protestant one – it was a simple as that. The Catholic one was in County Derry and the Protestant one in the adjoining county of Antrim, with only a couple of miles between them.

Portstewart was full of priests and brothers, who all seemed to stay in the Montagu Arms Hotel, near the Star of the Sea

Church, where the Kanes heard mass every morning before breakfast. One did not have to be in church at any particular time, for there were so many priests around that the whole morning was filled with mass. The Dominican Convent, formerly Montagu Castle, was surround by a high wall and dominated the scene from its lofty position on the cliff-top. A narrow path just outside the wall led round to the strand, where all the serious bathers had their dip. On rough days the breakers below would throw spray as high as the convent walls and make the cliff-walk a hazardous route to take, though timing one's run past the worst spots, in order to avoid the deluge, was a sport that Sean enjoyed.

Bathing in the freezing water at the strand was something he did not enjoy at all. Paddling in the small pool near the church was alright, but immersing one's whole body in the dashing waves was an entirely different matter. He tried to explain to his mother that the sea near Portstewart really was arctic, coming almost directly from Iceland and the North Pole. He offered to show it to her on a map, but she was adamant that sea-water cured just about everything and was really 'healthy'. She was not great at taking to the water herself, but would wade in to knee-depth, with skirt tucked in, and wash her face and arms.

She had now completed this first stage of the ritual and was ready to begin her encouragement of the shivering children. She caught Jenny by the arm and held her in the water while she cupped her other hand and soused the poor girl's back with the freezing Atlantic. Their sister's screams were too much for Sean and Eamonn, who turned and ran for the safety of the sand-dunes, not heeding the threats that followed them.

Lying in the sharp coarse grass of the dunes, they watched their other sisters' 'baptisms' below them at the water's edge.

Sean consoled himself by wondering why girls seemed better able than boys to withstand cold water. He would be blue and shaking after five minutes of it, while they could stay immersed with no sign of suffering. They all said one got used to it, but he had never attained that happy state and wouldn't particularly care if he never did.

Eamonn and himself spent the rest of the afternoon running up the sand-dunes: it was no easy task, as the dry sand crumbled and slipped away beneath their pounding bare feet. When they'd reach the top there was the glorious choice of sliding down or running until they fell headlong into the sand's yielding firmness. Once in a while they peeped over the top of the sand-dunes to see if the bathing ceremonies were complete; missing the dip was one thing, but they had no intention of missing tea as well. Sand and sea were great boys for putting an edge on the appetite!

They had their meals together at the small table in the bay window of Mrs McAloon's boarding house. It projected so much into the Promenade that it was a bit like having your meals on the public street. Bridie Kane knew a lot of people, and meeting friends and having a chat was a big part of her enjoyment of the holiday.

She insisted on good table manners from her children and was glad to have them isolated from the main table, lest they might transgress in front of the regular guests. Mrs McAloon was glad of the arrangement as well, for she had a special menu for the Kanes and it was tacitly understood that Bridie would not encourage overeating among the children on their Portstewart holiday.

Sean tried to take the last slice of bread from the plate as he left the table, but his mother spotted him.

'It's bad manners to empty all the plates and leave nothing behind,' she reminded him.

He felt like asking if it was good manners to let her very own child go to bed starving, but when he remembered the sand-dunes and the dip they had avoided in the afternoon, he thought it better to say nothing. If they met some of his mother's special friends 'doing the Prom' later in the evening they might be invited into the Italian restaurant for tea and cakes or perhaps ice-cream. He'd normally prefer ice-cream, but cakes could prove to be a better filler this evening. He began to feel good again.

After breakfast next morning they sat in a row on a wooden seat in the public shelter, staring mournfully out at the rain. Sean would have liked to go back to McAloon's, but that was impossible, because the beds had to be made and the rooms cleaned. What a bore, he thought: even in the shelter they were expected to behave themselves. Adults must have little to do when they can afford to spend so much time keeping us in check.

Chapter Four

The rain eased after tea and they took a bus to Portrush, where Barry's Amusements were the big attraction. Sean and Jenny paid their sixpence and stepped into the bumper car: visitors from England called them 'dodgems', but that name seemed to indicate a less aggressive approach to the business in hand than 'bumper'. If the car was used for bumping, then it should be called a bumper, Sean reasoned. He did the driving and Jenny did the squealing when they bumped another car or were themselves rammed. Their car refused to move after one such collision, but the friendly attendant in gym shoes jumped on behind and turned the wheel rapidly until the car swung round and headed for the centre of the arena again. Sean liked the smell of the sparks from the collector, which was attached to the top of each car-pole. The bumpers were great at any time of day, but there was an added dimension of excitement in the gathering dark of the evening as each loud crash was accompanied by its own individual flash of lightning from the meshed wire of the roof above them. There was no let-up in Jenny's screams and Sean wondered if his sister actually enjoyed having the life frightened out of her. When the man in charge pulled the main switch and all the cars drifted to a quiet stop, she refused to leave, even when the attendant came to collect money for the next round. Brid ran over with sixpence from his mother and away they went again. That was another thing he noticed – there seemed to be more money available in Portstewart than they ever had in Derry.

Sean could have stayed all night in Barry's, either rolling half-pennies on the big round table with all the numbers or trying to win presents with the little silver crane in the glass case. It was not getting his undivided attention this evening, since his mother had given him the job of keeping an eye on the weans while she had a few games of bingo. Brid and Jenny were in the process of making their fortune on the machine which emptied itself at you noisily if three little oranges finished up side by side when the whirring pictures stopped. The world and its granny would know they had just won, Sean thought, as Jenny's laugh came to him above the noise of the slot machines.

They left Barry's and went for a walk around Portrush. Holidaymakers here were noisier and happier than those in Portstewart. When they came to the lifeboat, his mother told them about the time it had come out too late to save their father's life. It was a story the older children knew well, as it was part of the family folklore that they had always known, with no recollection of when they had first been told.

Sean was four when his father died and now had only two memories of him. These he had kept renewing in his mind, so that his father would not entirely slip away from him. He thought of the Sunday after mass when his father had taken him and Brid down to see his ship's quarters. He remembered a small cramped place with a low roof that made his father stoop and a big cabinet with long drawers that he and Brid explored. That memory was clearer in his mind than the second vague recollection of his father coming home from sea, putting Sean up on his knee and giving him long pieces of paper, which he thought now might have been bus tickets, to play with. That was the earliest memory of all and Sean sometimes wondered if it had been really happened or was only in his imagination. It had to be true: he certainly wouldn't like to be Jenny or Eamonn or Mary, with no memories at all of their Daddy.

'When did Daddy die?' Eamonn asked.

Sean knew the answer to that and so did Jenny.

'You said we could get ice-cream if we left the bumpers that time, Mammy.' Jenny was determined that her mother would stick to her part of the bargain. Leaving the excitement of the little cars had been awful: even ice-cream would barely compensate her.

They went into Battisti's ice-cream parlour and were lucky to get a table all to themselves, with high-backed wooden seats on each side, closing them off from everyone else. They had a small vanilla ice-cream each in a glass dish, with a squirt of raspberry flavouring on top which ran down the sides and mixed with the ice-cream to form a pink pool in the bottom of the dish. If anything, the ice-cream in Portrush was even better than Yanarelli's in Derry. Sean let it melt in his mouth until its coldness gave him a pain along his forehead and behind his nose. He could not hold back a sharp cry, shut his eyes tightly and rubbed his forehead to get some ease. His mother offered him a sup of her tea, but Brid had no sympathy for him.

'That's a wild stupid thing to do,' she said severely, 'holding it in your mouth like that. You're supposed to swallow it – not suck it. Only put a wee bit in your mouth at a time and it won't happen.'

Eamonn was trying his hardest to get a foothold in the conversation, but no-one heeded his efforts until his mother quietened the others for him.

'What is it Eamonn?' she asked.

'Tell us about Daddy,' Eamonn said. He was determined to hear the story.

'Sure there's no good in talkin' about it now,' his mother sighed. 'What's to be must be.'

But they knew she would talk about it. The weans wanted to learn the details, while Brid, Sean and Jenny derived comfort hearing again a story they knew well. Sean was sure that in her heart his mother liked talking about it when the time was right. He could not imagine a better occasion than this, with all of them squeezed tightly together in their own little alcove, scraping the last goodness from Battisti's glass dishes.

'Well,' said his mother, 'the captain wanted to put the ship into Belfast so that he could be transferred directly to hospital, but your Daddy wouldn't hear of it. He knew he had appendicitis, but was willing to suffer on till they reached home in Coleraine.'

'The captain gave him whiskey,' Brid said.

'He did,' said her mother, 'and it was the very worst thing he could have done.'

Sean had heard before about the tide being too low at the mouth of the Bann to let their ship cross the Barmouth and dock in Coleraine. That was why they had to blow and blow for the lifeboat.

'That Portrush lifeboat didn't put out for ages,' she said. It was hard to know from her voice whether she was resigned or resentful.

When his father reached the hospital in Coleraine he already had a perforated appendix and a mere six days of life left in him. He was just thirty-six years of age, with a young wife and four children: the eldest, Brid, was five, Sean himself four, Jenny two and Eamonn, who was called after his father, not yet a year old. His youngest sister Mary was to be born six months later.

'Daddy sang when he was dying,' Sean said.

'Aye, he did so – *The Old Bog Road* and *The Road to the Isles*: my heart was sore listenin' to him. He was a grand singer and right and fond of the odd Scottish song that he had picked up when we lived in Glasgow.'

'Tell us about the time you were going back to Glasgow after I was born,' Jenny demanded.

'Well,' said her mother, 'I went on board at Derry quay very early that night and got the three of you off to sleep before we sailed, so that you wouldn't notice anything when we'd leave Lough Foyle and face into the rough seas away beyond Magilligan. The forecast that night was for high wind.

'We had a quiet night and when I looked out in the morning we were already berthed. I could hardly believe our luck and got the three of you dressed as quickly as I could, for I wanted to show our Glasgow neighbours the new Irish baby. It was only when I was walking down the gangplank that I recognised the familiar landmarks of the Guildhall and Craigavon bridge. I nearly fainted with the shock when I realised we were still in Derry: it had been too rough to put to sea the night before. Even though we had great neighbours in Glasgow, who were very kind to me when your Daddy was away on long European trips, I was happy when he took a job on a smaller boat and we made our home in Coleraine.'

Sean felt the old sadness creeping into her voice. That was the only snag about coming to Portrush – it awakened memories in his mother's mind of the first really happy period of her life and reminded her how it suddenly ended with the news that her husband had been rushed to hospital to fight with death. His struggle ended on the fourth day of January 1935, and they buried him in Drumsurn graveyard, a short distance from the hills of Kilhoyle, where he had been reared.

'He always said he'd like to be buried near the front door of Drumsurn church, where all the lads used to gather after mass to talk about football. It was a bit of a joke between us really, but I remembered it when the grave was being picked.'

She looked anxiously at them, biting her lower lip: 'I don't know how we would have survived if your Uncle Manny and Aunt Cassie hadn't brought us to Derry after the funeral. I just don't know at all.'

There was no more to be said and the ice-cream was done. His mother looked at her watch – it was the one she had got as an engagement present from Daddy and Sean knew it was the only bit of jewellery she had left now. He remembered bracelets and necklaces which somehow disappeared one by one, these last few years: he was sure that the tiny gold watch with the delicate hands and the expanding bracelet holding it on her wrist would not go the same way.

'Goodness, would you look at the time,' she said, bustling them out of the little alcove. 'We're goin' to miss the Portstewart bus if we don't run this minute.'

Chapter Five

Sean was sailing his boat in the paddling pool. It wasn't a bad little yacht at all, he thought, considering that it had been fashioned by Uncle Manny out of the leg of an old mahogany table which had broken, but it did not compare with the professional models that were cutting past it in the water, with their adjustable sails swinging to catch the wind and smoothly painted sides merging into a deep metal keel. His was flat-bottomed, unpainted and had a tiny sail, sewn around the mast by his mother. He waded out to where it drifted sideways and resolved to get a proper boat next year – one with an exotic name printed on the side of it.

He went back up along the beach to where his mother sat knitting on the steps leading up to the Promenade. Brid and Jenny were digging a tunnel in front of her. He pushed away the dry, powdery sand that formed a top layer on the beach and started to burrow into the wet sand, using only his hands. As he went deeper he turned the tunnel towards the others until his full arm was out of sight beneath him. He strained for the last few inches, hoping for the breakthrough into his sisters' tunnel. When it came at last, his shoulder was stuck in the entrance hole and his face pressed into the firm sand. They both laughed as his fingers found Jenny's, where the two tunnels joined.

Behind them on the steps a band of what his mother called Bible-thumpers had set up. He liked the sound of the harmonium and the kind face of the singer, a woman with a fresh country complexion. His mother told him to keep on playing in the sand and not mind what 'them Protestants' were saying. He couldn't help hearing that some of the hymns had lovely airs: one was full of impassioned pleas to come back to Jesus and he felt that the singer really meant it. Sean was confused: he always thought that Catholics were the ones who had never left Jesus.

It was not his first experience of this particular group, for they had been mounting a week-long campaign against his faith, with sand-castle competitions and racing on the beach. One had only to take part in their hymns to get a badge and be eligible for the competitions. On seeing the display of glittering prizes, he had been sorely tempted to succumb to their heathen advances and forget the faith of his forefathers – at least for a while!

It was James Murphy who first suggested going in for the fifty-yard dash. The Murphys were staying in McAloon's with them and the two mothers had struck up a friendship, just as their children had. James was older than Sean and laughed at his worries about what their parents would say.

'Just you leave it to me,' James said. 'I'll get us badges and we'll be in that race this very evenin' before tea.'

Sean could see him now behind the organ, pretending to sing and hoping that his own mother or Sean's wouldn't spot him. One minute he'd be singing his heart out and the next he'd be out of sight when his mother turned to look up at the Promenade. At last the group-leader pinned a badge on his shirt: James stopped singing in mid-verse and ran down to Sean to show him what he had got.

'I thought you were going to get me one as well,' said Sean.

'So I am,' answered James, 'if you'll swap shirts with me.'

James returned to a different point in the group around the organ and began his second performance. The badge was harder to acquire this time but he stuck to his task. They were announcing the fact that the races would be held just after the service and he was still badgeless. Sean saw him speaking to the group-leader before the last hymn. It struck him that his mother was right about the Murphys not being 'bird-mouthed'. He himself wouldn't have James's nerve. In fact he was beginning to have second thoughts about the race himself.

'Just don't say anything to your mother about it,' James advised him. 'My mother would go mad if she thought I was entered in a Protestant race, so I don't say a dicky-bird about it. You're not forgettin' the prize is a red yacht, are you?'

What a foolish question, Sean thought, and him after disobeying his mother and about to desert his religion to get his hands on it.

He saw his mother and Mrs Murphy gathering up their bits and pieces and calling the children to go back to Mrs McAloon's for tea. Sean and James made a big show of running on ahead but ducked into the ice-cream shop until the others had passed. They reached the beach again just in time for the start of the race.

The finishing tape was held by two ladies, near where the Kanes and Murphys had been playing in the sand, and the runners were lined up together at the other end. He stayed beside James, who had pushed his way into the centre of the twenty runners. Some of them were unhappy at the late intrusion, but they were smaller than James so they kept quiet. Sean bent over in his best professional manner, but he noticed that James was standing up straight with his eyes fixed on the starter.

'When I move, just go for that tape like the hammers of hell,' he muttered to Sean.

James was off and Sean followed him a fraction of a second before the starter shouted 'go'. It was hard to run in the soft sand, but he managed to keep up with James at first. He heard the pounding of other feet and panting at his right shoulder and knew he was about to be passed. He put on maximum pressure and stayed in front. James was only a yard ahead and the tape was near. He thought of the yacht and was gaining ground all the time. James looked sideways at him and stuck out his pumping elbows. He ran sideways to avoid them, knowing he was going to win, but his foot went deep into a sand-tunnel and he fell heavily, sticking out his hand to save himself. It double beneath him just as James breasted the tape to win.

He lay there, trying to get his breath back after the fall and ready to cry with the awful disappointment of it all. He didn't really blame James for sticking out his elbows: he'd have beaten him anyway, only for the tunnel-hole. The thought that he might have made the tunnel himself in the afternoon was too terrible to contemplate.

He tried to rise and felt a sudden weakness and pain in his right arm. He couldn't lift it without the help of his other arm. He knew he had done wrong and was being punished. What would he tell his mother?

James had the red yacht in his hands and his eyes were shining.

'Isn't she a smasher?' he asked. 'Will we try her out?'

Sean couldn't watch him, but made his way to the Promenade. Even before he reached McAloon's he could see the family eating in the bay window. He opened the dining-room door with his left hand and walked in.

'Where have you been till this time?' his mother asked severely. 'Mrs McAloon had your tea ready ages ago.'

'I think me arm's broke.' He felt the tears welling up in his eyes and couldn't blink them back. 'I can't lift it.'

He expected punishment but none came. His mother was softer and gentler than she had ever been towards him. Mrs McAloon said Pierre would know whether it was broken or not, so Pierre was called down from his attic room, where he had been getting ready for his evening show at the Summer Revels. He was billed as a French comedian and tight-rope artist, but had been born Rex Peden in Belfast and all his people were in the entertainment business. Everyone regarded him as an expert in bones, because he had broken most of his own at one time or another.

He was already dressed as a clown, with white painted eyes and big red lips. When he lifted Sean's arm he was surprisingly gentle, moving it this way and that to see what caused pain.

'Eet ees not broken,' he said, in his best French accent. 'Only a small sprain.'

He took Mrs Kane's headscarf and improvised a sling, knotting it behind Sean's neck. Then he dipped into a voluminous pocket and brought out a blue handkerchief with big white dots and bandaged the wrist.

Mrs McAloon brought in the tea and gave him a special place at the big table. He lifted the cup in his left hand and his mother fed him fish and bread.

'Cheer up,' said Pierre. 'I think you not die yet. I show you some-think.'

'He removed the metal cap from the sauce bottle and put in

on the table. Then he sat down opposite Sean and said, 'Tell me where you want eet to move,' indicating the top of the bottle.

Sean pointed to the left and the cap moved that way. Every command was obeyed and the little cap kept sliding on the table. Sean was laughing now and had almost forgotten his pain.

'As verry special favour I ah show you how eet ees done.' Said Pierre. 'All else leave room.'

They all went out and Pierre showed him the big magnet between his knees under the table. Sean tried it, but his legs were too short to reach up under the table.

'You'll do it when you are older,' Pierre told him. 'When your arm is better I'll teach you how to walk the tight-rope.'

Sean noticed that the exotic French accent had been replaced by a hard, down-to-earth Belfast one. The clown had disappeared, to reveal a different sort of man. A memory of his father flashed into Sean's mind and he wondered what it would be like if he were alive now.

His mother tucked him into bed that night and made him lie on his left side so as not to hurt the other arm. She told Eamonn to stay on his own side of the bed and not to be rolling over on his brother's sore arm. He was relieved that no-one had questioned him about how it had actually happened. He had Pierre to thank for that, with his talk and his tricks. He chuckled at the thought of him and Eamonn wanted to know what was so funny. Then he felt guilty again when he remembered the bible-thumpers and their prizes. Nobody could say he had actually taken part in a Protestant service. He worried about James though, as he had done so twice and had taken their prize.

His mother gave a last tuck to the bedclothes, tight in to the back of his neck and under his chin. 'If you've pain in the night come into our room,' she said. 'Maybe we should take you to the hospital in Derry tomorrow evening.'

With all the excitement he had forgotten that they were to go home tomorrow. He was going to miss this bedroom with its big water-jug set in the washing bowl and their own towel. At home there was barely room for their small bed, but here they had the luxury of a wardrobe, a chest of drawers and pictures of Portstewart on the walls. It would have been perfect, he thought, if there had been a view of the Promenade from the bedroom window and of the big breakers dashing against the rocks. The better-paying customers enjoyed that luxury.

Next day he decided to spend the last few hours before train-time over at the deep swimming pool, where a gala was in progress. The grace of the divers thrilled him, as they plummeted from the highest board and cut like knives in the water. Beyond the diving boards he could see the rock pools left by the receding tide. Eamonn had caught a fish there yesterday, with the rod, but Jenny maintained that it wasn't a fish at all, since it had claws and was a hideous green creature. Eamonn resented this insult to his first big catch and enquired sarcastically what a girl would know about fishing anyway.

Sean still wore the sling supporting his bandaged hand. In the privacy of the bedroom he had taken it off and found that he could move his arm quite well, but decided to keep in on: people seemed to be nicer when he wore it. He'd take it off in the train and then there'd be no question of going to the hospital in Derry. It was hard to accept that the holiday was nearly over.

He was looking forward to the greasy-pole competition. There were six local competitors taking part. The first wobbled his way out along the pole for only a few feet, before slithering helplessly into the water with a splash, and none of the others were any better. The man with the megaphone announced that the special guest star was to be none other than the famous French comic and tight-rope artiste extraordinaire – Pierre Renault from Paris. The crowd clapped when Pierre appeared in his clown's costume, carrying an enormous, gaily-coloured umbrella. He threw it up in the air, did a somersault and caught it again. When the applause subsided he put his foot on the greasy-pole and began to edge his way forward. He had already passed the half-way mark before he started to sway. He balanced himself with the umbrella and aimed again for the lonely end of the pole. Each time he faltered they gasped and each gasp seemed to spur him on. Sean willed him right out to the end. They cheered and clapped when he was securely poised there and Sean laughed with them at the exaggerated bow Pierre made to acknowledge the plaudits of his audience, before tossing away the umbrella and cheekily somersaulting into the water.

'Mammy said you're to come in this minute. We're all packed and ready to go.' Brid didn't like malingerers any more than his mother did.

He was glad to have missed the packing. There was nothing to bring back anyway – not a single thing. Brid and Jenny had lost all their Portrush gains in the Portstewart Amusement Arcade the very next day and Eamonn's fish had been thrown out. Mary had mislaid the tiny whistle, the only prize Sean had succeeded in extracting from the glass case with the silver crane: his mother was worried in case the child had swallowed it. He thought of his boat and was surprised to realise that he wasn't worried whether they had packed it or not. He filled up with disappointment at having nothing of Portstewart to take him with him.

'Empty the sand out of your shoes before we go in.' Brid reminded him.

He sat on the window-sill of McAloon's to perform the ritual for the last time, just as he had done it every day of the holiday, but something stopped him. He placed his foot carefully inside the shoe again and was happy to feel the crunch of sand when he wriggled his toes.

Chapter Six

There was not much room in the school-desks in Brother Sheehan's class. There were fifty pupils in fifth class and Sean Kane sat in the third row. Beside him was Liam Coyle from Buncrana. The low ceiling meant that the room was always stuffy and one couldn't see out of the steamed-up windows. He could hear the droning of the twelve-times table from Mr Cole's class behind him. They were in the same room but facing the other way.

The clock struck the hour and the twelve-times table stopped. The hinges of the desk-seats squeaked and squealed as they moved to let everybody stand up and face the statue of the Blessed Virgin on the side-wall.

'In ainm an Athar agus an Mhic agus an Spioraid Naoimh.' Brother Sheehan placed one hand on his chest and made the sign of the cross carefully with the other. They all mumbled dutifully so that he could see their lips and watch the precision of their hand movements. That was important.

Brother Sheehan seemed to enjoy his carefully enunciated Irish, as they blessed themselves every hour, on the hour. None of the other brothers used the national language. The Hail-Marys were in English today, but sometimes Brother Sheehan would try one in Irish. Sean had learned to follow it pretty closely himself and liked it. He watched a bead of moisture zig-zagging its way down the green painted wall beside the statue, leaving a wet trail behind to mark its passage. It joined another on the sweaty surface, increasing its speed as it searched for a bigger droplet to team up with.

'Sit down, Kane!'

He sat down.

It was composition day and they were to write about Saint Patrick. They were well prepared, for Brother Sheehan had read the life-story of the patron saint to them yesterday. It was getting near the seventeenth of March and their teacher liked to give them a topical subject to write on. Nothing was left to chance. Each student had to suggest a hard word and it would then be spelt out on the blackboard. No school-inspector was going to find shoddy work in their exercise books, not if Brother Sheehan could help it.

'Isn't that right?' he said, waving his strap at them. 'There will be no bad spelling in this class. I won't have it. Do ye hear that?' He gave the desk a stinging whack and they all winced.

He was already half-way along the first row in his quest for words to put on the blackboard. It was easy to think of 'Downpatrick' and 'Slemish' and 'Tara', but it was getting more difficult by the time his questioning reached the second row. One just had to have a word to give him or take the consequences.

Liam Coyle was in a highly agitated condition as Brother Sheehan's questions came nearer and nearer. He wished he had stayed at the primary school in Buncrana, even though he used to finish up near the bottom of the class there, in every examination. His mother was convinced that what he needed was discipline, so she sent him to the Brothers.

He would get the Lough Swilly bus early each morning in

Buncrana and travel the fifteen miles to Derry for his daily torture. Once he had spent the entire day in Brooke Park, returning school-less to Buncrana on the evening bus. But nothing ever worked out right for poor Liam: he was spotted by one of the teachers who was visiting the public library there and he paid dearly for his day of freedom.

Now he looked to Sean for help as the danger threatened.

'Give us a hard word,' he whispered in desperation.

Some devil entered Sean's mind and he replied 'Afghanistan'. It was a country he had discovered in his new atlas and he liked its long name.

'Afghanistan?' Even Liam had doubts about that one. 'What has that to do with Saint Patrick?'

'He used to go there on his holidays.'

There was no time left for further discussion. Brother Sheehan had reached the third row and was pointing at Liam.

'Next word,' he demanded.

'Please sir, Afghanistan.'

'What?' shouted the teacher and they could see the colour rising in his cheeks beneath the dark stubble.

Liam repeated the awful word.

'What has Afghanistan got to do with Saint Patrick?' asked Brother Sheehan. His voice was slow and deliberate, but it had an edge of steel.

'Please sir, he used to go there on his holidays.'

The class sniggered as Brother Sheehan scattered desks to get at him.

'Who told you that?' he screamed.

'P-Please s-sir, him,' stuttered Liam, pointing at Sean.

Sean was lifted by the sidelocks and suspended in the air like a beef sample. The pain at his ear and around the side of his head was awful. It was Brother Sheehan's favourite opening attack and he had attained a terrible expertise in its execution.

'I'll give you Afghanistan, you impudent pup.' The strap cut through the air and stung his flesh. On and on it went: there was no escape from the iron-grip on his sidelock.

Long after it was over his flesh still tingled where the sharp pain had been. He could see the homeboys sneaking looks at him when the teacher turned to the blackboard. They wanted to see how he was taking it. His hand shook as he wrote 'Saint Patrick' at the top of the page in his composition. The homeboys were well used to the strap. He'd show them.

He was sure, though, that one of them would be on his side. Jim Sweeney seemed different from the other homeboys. He came with them every morning, marching in a long line from the Termonbacca orphanage, wearing the same uniform and suffering the same pangs of hunger: his bare legs were just as raw from cold and undernourishment. But he could laugh and make friends.

Sean reached down into his schoolbag for the extra lunch his mother had put in for Jim. He kept his eye on Brother Sheehan's back as he slipped the package inside his shirt. He noticed the line of melted butter seeping through the brown paper: she must have forgotten the greaseproof wrapping. Jim wouldn't be too worried about that.

Then it was toilet time. They filed out of the classroom and formed a line outside, at the top of the steps. When Brother Sheehan gave the word they started down towards the lower yard.

They passed the woodwork room belonging to the Technical

School on their way and Sean stared in. He saw his cousin Harry working at a vice, with wood-shavings all around him. He'd have given anything to be his cousin, but it was only 'Tech' boys who did woodwork. Harry waved out at him but Sean saw Brother Sheehan staring, so he didn't respond. He knew Jim was somewhere behind him in the line but there was no way of getting the lunch to him. Giving lunches to homeboys was one of Brother Sheehan's reserved sins.

The fresh air was great after the stuffiness of the classroom. As he sucked it into his lungs he felt a calmness replacing the previous turmoil. They turned the corner into the long 'walk'. It had a dangling chain suspended between iron stakes on one side and a row of iron railings on the other. Through them he could see down into the toilets, in the corner of the concreted yard. The houses of Lecky Road were separated from the school by a high wall. He checked to see where Brother Sheehan was and swung the chain noisily. He had forgotten to bless himself as he passed the statue of Our Lady in the glass case. That was a lucky escape, he thought, as Brother Sheehan turned the corner.

'Class, halt,' the teacher shouted.

They went into the toilet in groups of six, while Brother Sheehan stood at the entrance, where he could see inside and yet keep an eye on the main group up on the 'walk'.

'Six more,' he shouted. As they approached the toilet Sean glanced back and saw that Jim was in the next group. The smell inside was terrible: it was always worse on a dry day. He stood in the position at the slate urinal and tried not to think about the putrid crust that covered everything. He stared straight in front of him as he peed. He knew better than to look left or right at his companions or even down at himself. The Brothers didn't like that. Maybe a necessary glance as you shook it and replaced it, but no more.

He stood there until the other five were going out. When he heard 'Next six' he unbuttoned his shirt and took out the lunch. As he turned to face the door he put the package behind his back and pretended to be still buttoning-up.

The next group were already running in before Sean was spotted. Jim took the lunch from him and kept moving towards the urinal.

'Come out, Kane,' the teacher shouted. 'What were you at in there?'

Sean ducked to avoid the blow and ran up to join the line. He'd have to watch himself with Brother Sheehan today. He was still on the warpath after yesterday's big blow-up with the homeboys.

It had all started when a Buncrana fellow reported that his tea-money had been stolen out of his gaberdine during lunchtime. Brother Sheehan decided that it had to be one of the boys from the orphanage who had taken the money, so he assembled all the homeboys in the school and lined them around the walls of the double classroom.

'Some of ye stole that money and it must be given back.' He bent and unbent the strap in his hand as he spoke. 'Do ye hear me?'

No-one spoke, but they jumped as he brought the strap down on the desk with all his strength.

'Did you take it?' he asked the first homeboy.

'No sir.'

He got the same answer from each of them in turn.

Both classes had by now given up all pretence of study and were watching to see what would happen next. Even Mr Cole stopped writing on his blackboard, put the chalk on the little shelf and clapped its dust off his hands. He adjusted his horn-rimmed spectacles on his nose with his left index finger and rubbed his hand over his mouth. It was a habit he had when he wasn't pleased. Sean had not seen it for a long time.

'Well, I'll soon find out who took it.' Brother Sheehan rolled up his sleeve as he spoke and turned again to the first homeboy. 'Maybe this will beat the truth out of ye.'

The bigger boys took their six-a-piece calmly enough, but one of the younger fellows was crying after three and pulled back his hand. The strap zinged on at speed and struck the teacher's own knee. Sean felt really sorry for the young homeboy then: Brother Sheehan's control had disappeared and the last venomous strike of the strap caught the young fellow on the wrist. Brother Sheehan had no intention of being foiled again. He pushed the crying lad aside and went for the next victim. Sean could hear the teacher's sharp expulsion of breath each time he brought down the strap: he had never before seen anyone so furious.

He was frightened now – afraid of Brother Sheehan and afraid of his strap – afraid to think about who had taken the money. Maybe he had taken it himself or maybe Liam had it. He knew for certain Jim wouldn't have taken it, but there he was in front of them, doubled up in agony under the statue of the Blessed Virgin, trying to squeeze the pain out of red swollen hands and probably thinking they were all against him. Sean was sick in his stomach and ashamed – the shame was the worst part of it. He couldn't face Jim after this.

It stopped at last and Brother Sheehan threw back the lock of black hair that hung down over one eye. He reached for breath to speak and could hardly find it. Beads of sweat rolled into the bushy eyebrows and the eyes seemed bigger than ever in his red face.

'Well,' he gasped, 'are ye going to own up now?'

There was a whiteness around his mouth from the pressure of his tightly closed lips as he looked around the classroom. No-one spoke. Sean thought Mr Cole was about to say something, but at that moment Brother Sheehan turned to the first home-boy.

'We'll soon settle this.' He raised the strap and pulled the lad towards him by the wrist, swung him around behind, so that only his arm could be seen in front of the Brother's soutane and then clamped the boy's thin arm beneath the Brotherly elbow. As the blows began to rain down the clock struck. Brother Sheehan paid it no attention.

From the other end of the room they heard Mr Cole's light voice: 'In the name of the Father and of the Son and of the Holy Ghost.'

Brother Sheehan looked up in surprise. Prayers were his job.

While they were answering the first Hail Mary, Mr Cole made his way down the room and stood beside Brother Sheehan to give out the second one. As they answered it, Sean could see Mr Cole whispering urgently to Brother Sheehan. As they answered the third Hail Mary, Brother Sheehan put the strap in his pocket, turned quickly and went out the door. Sean saw him passing the window on his way to the Brothers' house.

Mr Cole waited until the squeaking of the seats had subsided before he spoke.

'Get out your readers and do a sentence each, from the top of page twenty-six. Will my class turn back around to their own blackboard and do the twelve-times table. Start now.'

The homeboys watched and waited to see what their fate was to be. They knew that Mr Cole was not the enemy.

'Homeboys, go back to your own classes.'

As he watched them go out he couldn't help thinking of his Aunt's terrier, which always expected a beating. Mr Cole let the two classes out early that evening. Sean went down the 'walk' with Charlie and Danny. Being let out early meant that he had no chance of seeing Jim, who had to march in line with the other homeboys at four o'clock. He was sorry about that.

Nobody referred to what had happened in class. He could feel Charlie's anger the whole way along Lecky Road and Rossville Street, before they parted company at Little James's Street. Danny and himself turned down the Strand Road for the long walk to Pennyburn.

'The Christians is a wild funny school,' Danny said.

Chapter Seven

The other altar-boys were having a slipper fight in their long, narrow changing room before last mass. Sean could hear them as soon as he mounted the steps to the sacristy. He had his own slippers rolled inside the white surplice under his arm. The noise subsided as he opened the door quickly. He knew they'd think it was Father Chapman, who was a deeply religious man. He liked to compose himself in prayer before mass, but the noise of flying slippers hitting the walls next door would often bring him running in angrily.

Barney Mackin, the chief altar-boy, came hurrying in from the altar, where he had just left the wine and water cruets.

'Who's on candles today?'

Danny put his hand up to his mouth: 'God, I forgot it was me.'

'Well, get a taper and be out there quick: we're goin' on the altar in a minute.'

Lighting candles for a weekday mass was no trouble at all since they only lit two small ones down at altar level, but late mass on a Sunday was different: all six big candles in the brass holders high up at the back had to be done.

'Give us a hand wi' the candles, Sean,' Danny asked.

They found two taper stumps on the window sill and stuck them into the end of the long lighters, just behind the brass snuffers. They knocked on Father Chapman's door and entered.

He had on the white robe, pulled tightly in at the waist with a cord, and was reaching for the green vestments which had been left ready on top of the pinewood cabinet.

'Well?' he said, not liking a disturbance.

'Could we have a light, Father?' Danny had on his 'innocent' face as he spoke.

'The matches are on that shelf. I thought I said last week that candles were to be lit early on a Sunday.'

The match broke on the box as Sean tried to light it, and fell to the ground, still flaming. Fr Chapman rushed across and stamped furiously on it.

'Give us those,' he said impatiently, snapping the box from Sean's hand. 'Bend the tapers away from the snuffer or there'll be no candles lit today.'

Barney Mackin opened the door for them and out they strode, side by side, carrying the lighters like rifles, but walking slowly, lest the draught extinguish them.

Sean hadn't expected the church to be so full, and they all seemed to be staring at him. His legs began to feel funny and he didn't know whether he should swing his free arm or not. He could see Danny's arm swinging, but couldn't get into time with it. It was ages before they reached the altar and genuflected together. He felt that one shoulder was higher than the other as he walked up the marble steps and round the back of the altar. This was his first time on Sunday candles and they seemed very high, even when he had mounted the back steps.

They had five candles lit at last, but Sean had failed with the sixth. He stretched as high as he could and rubbed the lighted taper back and forth on the distant top of the candle. He had no view of it himself, but Danny was standing back, watching closely for the first little glimmer of light. 'No good,' he whispered, shaking his head.

Sean saw his aunt down there, looking up at him, and Mrs Friel. Jim Meenan from Messines Park was pointing him out to his father. He had never liked that young fellow. Was nobody praying down there, he wondered, as he kept moving the light across the top of the candle. 'Please light … please,' he muttered, but the candle did not respond.

Barney Mackin came bustling out to the altar.

'Come down outa that,' he said in a whisper that could be heard half-way down the church.

Barney's height gave him an advantage with the big candles and this one lit up as soon as he touched it. Sean felt stupid.

'Father Chapman's leppin' in there,' Barney said, as he pushed Sean in front of him towards the sacristy door.

When he opened it he saw the altar boys in pairs, facing him and ready to go out for mass.

'You be on the door,' Barney Mackin said to him. He liked giving orders.

Sean stood there facing them all, his hand on the door-handle, ready to swing it wide open at a signal from the priest. Fr Chapman was behind Barney Mackin, adjusting his biretta on his head. He didn't look happy.

But nobody could say the same about Danny. He had squeezed into the front row of altar boys and was making funny faces at Sean. He knew that Fr Chapman couldn't see him, so he got bolder and bolder.

Fr Chapman was issuing his final instructions.

'Walk out slowly now and keep together: wait until I turn back to face the altar at the Orate Fratres before you answer and …'

Danny had both hands up to his face, but with elbows pushed into his stomach so that Fr Chapman wouldn't notice anything from behind. His fingers pulled the skin down from his eyes until the inner redness appeared beneath the big eyeballs and his thumbs pushed down his lower lip and the sides of his mouth. He stuck out his tongue and Sean's laugh exploded into Fr Chapman's instructions.

The priest was on to him like a dog to a rabbit. His big hands came down on the curly hair and clenched firmly. He shook Sean backwards and forwards in fury until the biretta fell to the ground. Danny picked it up and almost pushed it into the priest's hands. Sean's spinning head was glad of the relief. Fr Chapman replaced the shaking biretta on his head and gave the signal with a curt nod. He swung the door open and they all filed out. Sean followed them and shut the door. Why had he laughed in there?

The long prayers before mass were over at last and the Latin had begun. 'Introibo ad altare Dei,' intoned the priest and six young voices raced through the garbled reply: 'Damn quell toffee cat: you've a tutta may.'

He found himself thinking of the day Brother Sheehan heard about himself and Danny having started to serve mass in Pennyburn. He brought them out in front of the class so that everybody could enjoy the Latin, close up, as it were. He himself would be the priest and Sean and Danny were to answer him.

They heard the familiar 'in tree bill tarry day' and they responded at speed with 'damn quell toffee cat: you've a tutta may'. This was well-trodden ground.

Brother Sheehan looked at them in surprise before he gave out the next priest's piece, beginning 'you'd a calmy days…' They both relaxed and waited for their next cue at the end of it: 'ate a low so, hairy may.'

Sean always liked the nice long response to that one as it gave the altar boys time to get together and speed out the Latin. Danny and himself were beginning to enjoy the limelight as they answered.

'Queer two's days. Forty chewed a may. Quarry may plisty ate quarry: this is in shay dough. Dumb fidget main meek us.'

'That's enough,' Brother Sheehan said, closing his missal with a snap. 'Who taught you that gibberish?'

Their Latin teacher was Aidan Barry, who had learned it by rote from an older altar-boy, who in turn had learned it from Sean's cousin when St Patrick's Church, Pennyburn, first opened some ten years previously. His cousin had been an altar boy in St Eugene's Cathedral before that, so they were all quite proud of their long Latin tradition.

Sean always thought they sounded great at mass, with up to ten of them spitting it out at speed as a machine-gun might have done.

Father O'Loughlin, a very gentle and understanding person, didn't wait for them and they didn't wait for him – both parties had a job to do and each got on with it, as independently as possible. The priest was responsible for his own pronunciation and they were responsible for theirs. But Brother Sheehan did not share this tolerant approach and started giving them regular lessons in correct Latin.

'We can't say it like that, Sean,' Danny said later, shaking his head. 'They'll say we're stuck-up.'

Sean agreed with him, so they clung to the Pennyburn Latin tradition.

There were various jobs to be done after mass. He helped Danny put out the candles, but there was an ulterior motive for that. He had to see if old Mr O'Brien, the solicitor, was in the church.

Snuffing out the big candles was a lot easier than lighting them. As he quenched the last one he allowed himself to look across towards Out Lady's altar, with its rows of burning candles. His mother said that every one of them was a prayer. He could see the white head of Mr O'Brien bent in meditation. He was in his usual seat, about a dozen rows back. He would be praying there for another ten minutes at least. There was no hurry.

When they went into the sacristy Mrs Logan was there, trying to find out who had stuffed her son's immaculate white surplice up the chimney.

The Logans lived in Duncreggan Road and were a cut above average. Hugh had become an altar-boy at the same time as Sean and Danny, but things didn't work out well for him. The altar-boys from Governor Road and Phillip Street didn't like him. Maybe it was his carefully-polished shoes and clean hands. Sean himself could see no good reason for their active dislike of him, but Danny put his finger on it when he said, 'That Logan is a wild Protestant-lookin' fella.'

More than anything else, his shining-white starched surplice seemed to attract their wrath. It was the product of hours of loving care by a devoted mother. Twice it had been down the toilet in the little room beside them and now Mrs Logan had found it covered in black soot in the chimney of the altar-boys' room.

As Sean replaced the candle-lighter in the long cupboard, he was glad to hear Fr Chapman telling her to come outside: only altar-boys and himself were allowed into that room. Anyway, she should have known better than to come disturbing a priest, but particularly Fr Chapman, after last mass on a Sunday. Hadn't he been fasting since last night? The priest might even eat the poor woman!

They were all in a hurry to get out now, in case she came back. Danny was pulling off his soutane.

'Are you comin' home, Sean?'

'No,' he said, 'I have to put fresh candles out in the candelabra. You go on yourself.'

'I'll give you a hand and we'll go out the main door afterwards, so that she won't see us.'

That was just what Sean did not want, but Danny already had lifted out a packet of new candles.

'Fr Chapman told me not to put them out until he came back.' Sean hoped his black lie sounded convincing. 'You run on Danny and I'll see you this evening at Devotions.'

Danny put the candles down on the window-sill and ran out. As soon as Sean heard the bang of the outside door he peeped into the church, through the narrow slit at the side of the polished wooden door.

Mr O'Brien was still there, but seemed to be gathering up his rosary and prayer-books. Sean let the door shut quietly and went back to get the two packets of candles. He put his knee up against the wall to support the candles as he carefully opened the narrowest slit in the doorway.

Mr O'Brien came slowly out of the seat, genuflected right down, bent his head and carefully blessed himself. For an awful moment Sean thought he was turning to leave the church, instead of moving up the aisle as usual to light a candle to the Blessed Virgin.

He let the door close quietly again, hoisted the two packets securely under his arm, counted up to ten and opened the door, making as much noise as he could with the handle.

Mr O'Brien had reached Our Lady's altar by the time Sean was opening the low brass gates at the altar-rail. He left them open behind him when he saw that his quarry was already looking inside the candelabra for a candle and searching his pocket for the money to pay for it.

Sean recognised the right moment and smiled at Mr O'Brien, while he unwrapped his first packet of candles. He busied himself then, filling up the depleted box with new candles. As he turned for the second packet he heard the money clinking in the candelabra slot. He had the packet opened when Mr O'Brien squeezed a sixpence into his hand and smiled. Sean's heart jumped and he gasped with delight: not, mind you, with surprise, since it was the third time this had happened in three visits to the candelabra. He had not expected it the first time, of course, but he liked to remember what his mother was always saying about God helping those who helped themselves.

He could see Mr O'Brien praying earnestly to God for his intentions. Sean really did hope that the good man would get what he wanted, but maybe not for a while yet!

Chapter Eight

It was Aunt Cassie who told Sean that war had been declared. She let him in after he had been rattling her back door for ages. The news was still blaring out on the wireless as they crossed the yard.

It was one of those boring days when there was nothing to do and none of his friends were out playing on the Crescent. He had called for Fred, but his mother said sternly that he wasn't going to get out until all his sums were finished and that was all about it.

He liked his Aunt's house: for one thing, they had a nice brown piano which some of his cousins played and for another, he'd sometimes find a comic behind the cushion on the sofa, though his Aunt didn't really agree with comics. The only thing he disliked about the sofa was the sharp horse-hair which stuck out through the black covering and stung his legs whenever he moved. He really preferred the softness of their own green sofa at home, but then Aunt Cassie always had biscuits and they made the sitting easier. She put a plate of them on the sofa beside him now and a glass of sparkling lemonade in his hand. He watched the bubbles rising in it, for a little while, so that she wouldn't think he was too greedy and had no manners.

'Drink up,' she said and began to tell him the news about Hitler. 'But don't fret,' she declared, 'England will soon halt that boy's gallop.'

Aunt Cassie had more confidence in England than his mother showed: they all knew that his Aunt regarded her younger sister as a bit of a rebel in these matters.

He thought he should leave the last biscuit on the plate, but was glad that Aunt Cassie pushed it into his hand when she took the place and glass from him, before washing them at the sink in the scullery. She was always on the go.

He went into the parlour and started to pick out *O'Donnell Abu* on the piano. It was a song they had all learned for the school excursion to Donegal. He sang it to himself as his fingers moved on the keys: 'Proudly the note of the trumpet is sounding'. It was easy as far as 'trumpet', but he had difficulty in finding the note that the tune leaped to then. It took him a few goes, but he got it eventually. He'd have it all in no time.

The top of the piano carried photographs of the family and there was a big one in a gilt frame above the fireplace. It showed a young priest who was a distant cousin of his mother and his Aunt Cassie.

He thought about trying out *The Soldier's Song* on the piano, but decided against it when he remembered his Aunt in the scullery and her Protestant Meadowbank neighbours on each side. None of them would be pleased to hear the Irish national anthem, particularly on the day that was in it.

He looked out. How lucky his cousins were to be able to see right across the Crescent from their own front window. Imagine being able to see Mackey's from his own house. Fred came out his front door and walked down the steps. He bounced a ball in front of him as he ambled along the Crescent towards Meadowbank.

He started to throw it against Miss Mooney's side-gable.

Hers was a Meadowbank house but the side-gable was in Richmond. It was where they played all the ball games. Fred was a good thrower and a good catcher too. Sean knocked as hard as he could on the window, but to no avail. He was just trying to open it when Miss Mooney appeared at her door across the Avenue. She was very agitated and Sean knew what she was going to say: they had heard it so many times before.

'Gwon outa that, or I'll get the police on you.'

Fred's father was a policeman, so he didn't think it a big threat, but he put the ball safely in his pocket, nevertheless, in case she tried to take it from him.

'Gwon now.' She shooed him away with a wave of her hand, like someone swatting a troublesome fly, and went into her house again. He stood there, not knowing if he should risk a few more balls on the gable.

Sean stuck his head out the open window. 'Come 'ere a minute Fred, till I tell you the news.'

'What news?' Fred shouted back, but stayed where he was.

'You have to come over here or I won't tell you.'

Fred crossed Meadowbank. 'Tell us then,' he said expectantly.

'Hitler has declared war,' said Sean and he watched closely to see the effect of his big news.

'Sure that's stale,' Fred replied. 'Me da told us hours ago. Everybody in the Crescent knows it.'

'Oh,' said Sean and he pulled down the window in his disappointment. His mother had been right when she talked about 'them oul policemen knowin' all your business.'

Workmen had started to level a site for an air-raid shelter behind Miss Mooney's house. Sean was shocked to see that they had cut away half of Strawberry Hill to make room for it. That surely was a sacrilege. To the builders, Strawberry Hill might have seemed only a slight rise in the general ground level, but it was where the gang always held the important meetings to declare war or make peace. Sean and Eamonn belonged to the Richmond Crescent gang and felt the insult of the desecration as deeply as the others.

It was on Strawberry Hill that he had tried to fasten Sue Mackey's new identification bracelet on her wrist last week. They were all the rage now, since Hitler had declared war and were supposed to be useful in the event of a German air-raid: you could get one in Woolworth's and have your name printed on it for half-a-crown. He tingled with happiness as he kept trying to fasten it on her freckled arm. He hoped nobody was watching him from a window across the street, but Sue didn't care. She laughed at him, looking straight into his eyes. She wasn't shy like a Catholic girl.

'I can't,' he said. 'It won't go on your wrist.'

He knew she was looking at him again so he concentrated his gaze on the bracelet.

'Do you want it?' she asked.

'What,' he said, not looking up.

'My bracelet,' she answered. 'Do you want my bracelet?'

'For keeps?' He was trying to keep his voice level as he spoke.

He read her name – Susan Helen Elizabeth Mackey. Her family obviously wasn't taking any chances on losing her, he thought. He liked being near her, even if it did get him confused.

The building of the shelter went ahead and there was nothing they could do about it. Meadowbank had two concrete shelters and they built a brick one at the bottom of Barry Street. His mother said the family would be safer under the stairs, so she put an old mattress in there. Whenever the whooping siren sounded the air-raid warning, their neighbours, the Smiths, would come in by the back door so that nobody would see them and all would squeeze into the tiny space under the stairs. Mrs Smith was not a thin woman and her husband was tall. After half-an-hour in the stuffy darkness Sean was glad to come out when the long all-clear siren blew. He was beginning to realise that death from suffocation was far more likely than death from a German bomb.

War was bringing prosperity to Derry. Hundreds of British soldiers and sailors had moved into Ebrington Barracks, over in the Waterside, and had started to spend their money in the Derry shops: Fred said he'd heard that they were even giving cash to some of the Derry girls but, for some reason, his mother thought that wasn't right.

Sometimes they'd see a sailor and a girl going into the deserted billiard room at the bottom of the lane: they'd often find what looked like old white balloons in there the following morning. Jim Deeney, who was in Sean's class, said he knew what they were for, but when he told them they knew he was only fibbing. Nobody would believe his ridiculous version of what they did with them. Sean thought it all a very funny business.

Derry quay was lined with the Navy's grey-blue ships – destroyers and corvettes, with large painted numbers on their hulls. According to Jim's father they were assembling for a convoy, but it was supposed to be a secret. Everybody in Derry discussed the Navy's business in minute detail, for there was plenty of information available and no-one paid too much attention to the big posters that were going up on the Strand Road billboards with the warning 'Careless Talk Costs Lives'.

Derry was pushing its way out of a pre-war obscurity and into the international scene. Sean and his mother listened to Lord Haw-Haw's broadcast one night and heard him telling the British Navy to come out from behind the Golden Teapot, or Germany would blast them out of it. Sean knew what he meant: the golden teapot hung outside McCullough's shop in Waterloo Place and the ships were crowded in the docks behind it. It was exciting to think that Germany seemed to know so much about Derry. He just hoped the anti-aircraft gun on top of Bryce and Weston's factory would frighten away any Germans who succeeded in avoiding the barrage balloons that ringed the Derry sky.

His mother took in a lodger. He was Chief Petty Officer Pearson, a big fat 'regular' sailor who despised all the fresh young officers who had just been recruited into His Majesty's Navy for the war and would run away again as soon as peace came. Pearson had been a navyman all his life. Sean enjoyed listening to his stories of sea-battles and sinkings. He had been shipwrecked once in the Atlantic and spent a full day in the sea before he was picked up. His big laugh filled the kitchen as he told them about the raw young sailors who had started to swim and were never heard of again. He attributed his own survival to the high 'blubber percentage' of his body and to his laziness in not trying to swim the Atlantic to safety. He was quite content to wait for the Royal Navy to find him – which they did eventually. Another enormous laugh shook his whole body, quivering all the layers of fat: tears streamed from eyes that were half-closed by the puffy flesh of his cheeks.

Christmas came and Pearson spent it with them. He brought

extra goodies from the ship – things they hadn't seen since the start of rationing. Sean was suffering for a surfeit of chocolate and fruit-cake by the time his mother switched on the BBC to hear the King's speech at three o'clock. She had already warned them all to be quiet and respectful while the King was speaking. Sean found it all a bit boring: the monarch had a bad speech impediment and would keep them waiting for what seemed minutes on end, before completing a single word or phrase. But the family knew better than to say anything about it in the presence of an English naval officer. As the monarch struggled to pass greetings to his loyal subjects around the world, this Chief Petty Officer in the King's Navy turned towards the wireless and addressed his sovereign with an unexpected familiarity: 'Cough it up then, Georgie – cough it up, boy.'

Eamonn and Sean were keen on fishing, but the recent closing of the dry-dock area behind the Swilly station took away one of their best spots. It was in there they had caught two flat-fish once. His mother wouldn't have anything to do with them when she heard they had come from the Foyle, but Sean cleaned them out himself and then fried them in the scullery when she had gone up the town shopping. You'd often get eels in there as well, but they'd leave your hooks and line all tangled up in a slimy mess. It might be ages before you'd realise they were on the line, as they didn't give the quick jerk of a hooked fish but would begin a slow series of twists and turns in their efforts to free themselves. But there was no longer any point in thinking about sitting happily at the end of the dry-dock. Their quiet fishing spot had become a hive of activity and top security, as carpenters, welders and riveters worked night and day to keep the British fleet in command of the North-West Approaches. Sean had often heard them talking about the 'Approaches'. He had no clear idea what they were, but he did know they had put an end to his hopes of more flat-fish.

His mother wanted to know why they wouldn't go fishing in a nice clean country river instead of in the filthy Foyle. That was when they decided to try the river Faughan out at Drumahoe. They were up early on a Saturday morning and digging worms in the far field before nine o'clock. When the cocoa tins were nearly full of good specimens, Sean threw some clay on top of them and grass, 'just to keep them alive'. They made a few holes in the lid with a nail, because they always did that: he wondered how worms managed for air when they were deep in the ground.

They took a bus to the Waterside and that gave them a great start on the journey. It seemed strange to be going beyond the bus terminus and taking the road marked 'Dungiven'. That was the way Mr McAdoo took them in his car last year when they went to Aunt Maggie's place in the country. But Drumahoe was only three miles out the road and the Faughan was supposed to be full of fish.

They fished and fished, but no fish came.

'It's too bright,' Eamonn said.

They moved to a darker spot beneath an overhanging tree.

'This is just right,' Eamonn said, giving the rod a big swing. The hook caught high in the branches and no amount of jerking would shift it. He cut the line and put on new gut and hooks.

'Are you hungry?' said Sean.

'Starvin'. Me belly thinks me throat's cut,' was the reply.

He took out the sandwiches while Eamonn set the lines, putting a big stone on each rod. He was clearly expecting a monster, thought Sean. It was a real pet of a day: they listened to the trout plopping in the river, only yards from the rods.

'Maybe the hooks are too big, Sean.'

'Aye. Maybe.'

The flies were collecting around them as they ate. Sean jumped up and shook himself to avoid them. Flies always gave him the shivers, particularly the big ones you'd find by the river.

'It might be better lower down,' he said.

Eamonn followed him towards the bridge. They could see an odd car passing on the Derry Road. An Army lorry went past and the soldiers waved to them.

'Them's salmon hooks,' said Sean, with an air of finality. 'You'll never catch trout with those big things.'

'Maybe we should get trout hooks and come back some other day,' Eamonn said hopefully.

They tidied up their gear and made their way along the bank until they reached the bridge. The evening rise was on and the fish were jumping furiously as he followed Eamonn over the barbed wire and on to the Derry Road. He heard the enormous splash of a salmon and was sure Eamonn had heard it too, but neither of them mentioned it.

They spent their last pennies on chewing-gum, so they had to walk all the way home. When they reached the Strand Road at last, they turned right to walk down the quay. It was always far more interesting than being on the main road. He'd be able to collect some grain for Gallan's pigeons too.

A dock policeman spoke to them. 'Are you naval officers?' he asked.

'No, we're not,' Sean answered. He couldn't help feeling a certain elation that a dock 'horney' had mistaken them for officers. It was some compensation for the long walk.

'Don't you know that only naval personnel and authorised people are allowed on the quay now?'

It took some time for them to realise the awfulness of the new situation. As they turned to leave, Sean could feel the utter loneliness of a quay that wouldn't belong to them any more.

'Well, damn Hitler anyway,' Eamonn said.

Chapter Nine

As they walked along the Strand Road, Sean wondered if he should try to forget all about the quay. They passed Lower Clarendon Street and both of them automatically looked right to see what was happening down there on the docks. The grain ship was being unloaded and he could see the dockers, each with a big long bag balanced on his right shoulder, running to the waiting lorry to be rid of his burden. It was a sight he had seen so many times before, but he never tired of watching the skilful flick of the shoulder as each docker let the bag empty out in a cloud of dust, above a stream of golden grain. He thought about Nick Gallan's pigeons and wondered what would happen to them now.

He was really sorry for Eamonn, who had only recently been allowed to go up the quay by himself. Before that, the weans had always to be accompanied by himself, Brid or Jenny. A dock policeman rounded the corner and came towards them. Surely he wouldn't try to stop them looking in from the Strand Road.

'Come on Eamonn: let's get home.'

He remembered the big Spanish ship that had lain at anchor in the Foyle, while the Spaniards fought among themselves at home. It hadn't been allowed to leave Derry for years and had difficulty getting its engines going again when it finally departed. Sean couldn't remember when it first came, but he could certainly recall the fuss when it left and the crowds up the quay watching it. He heard his cousins saying then that it had a new crew on board. Eamonn was too young to remember that.

And his Uncle Joe from America: Derry quay always made him think of Joe, but that was before the war. It wasn't a happy memory.

The family regarded him as a rich uncle, since he had a 'store' in Connecticut and nobody else in the family was in commercial life. Sean very much wanted to meet his father's elder brother, just to see what he was like.

Bridie Kane had gone to a lot of trouble to ensure that her American brother-in-law would feel welcome. Things appeared on the table that the children had never seen before – even the oil-cloth covering was replaced by a linen tablecloth. Sean thought this a bad idea: if he spilled soup or tea on the oilcloth it was a simple matter to hold up the edges so that the liquid wouldn't run and his mother could soak it up on a dishcloth. Her starched white linen tablecloth, a carefully preserved wedding present, presented an entirely different problem and made Sean nervous in case he should make a blunder. He did not get the opportunity, since Uncle Joe ate alone, with the family seated in a row on the sofa, alongside the table, watching him carefully and noting not only what he ate, but more particularly, what he did not consume. No-one spoke, for their mother had warned them beforehand to be absolutely quiet and her stern glance reinforced the earlier warning each time she emerged from the scullery with more food.

Five pairs of eyes following his every mouthful was beginning to make Joe feel a bit uncomfortable. He swivelled round in his chair to face the sofa. He looked at Jenny who sat in the middle.

'What grade are you in?

Jenny stared at him and he repeated the question with the

same result. Her mother came in with the coffee, a new concoction from what looked like a sauce-bottle. She was flustered after her first ever coffee-making session.

'Did you not hear your uncle asking you a question?' she asked sharply. Jenny nodded.

'Well,' said her mother, 'don't just sit there like a stummy: have you no mouth on you?'

Jenny blushed, opened her lips to speak and remembered her mother's earlier warning.

The more he thought about all the fuss for his Uncle Joe, the funnier it seemed to Sean. Even though their uncle had been half a lifetime in the States, wore coloured ties and spoke with a rich American accent, he was still his father's brother, born and bred in Kilhoyle, far from coffee in small cups and bowls of fresh fruit on the table for every meal. The poor man never actually ate the fruit himself – the family did it for him, in a headlong dash to the table, just as the kitchen door closed behind him.

The night before he left, Joe talked about Kilhoyle and the times they'd had there, about football and his father. Until then, Sean had not known that his father had travelled much of America and had stayed for a time in Joe's house there. Would Sean like to come to America and live there? He wasn't sure if Joe meant it or not: his mother was smiling.

Joe set off next day to take the 'tender' to Moville and board the transatlantic liner there. About an hour after he left Sean began to have second thoughts. The house seemed lonely without his uncle and everything was very ordinary again. His mother told him to stop sulking and go out and chop firewood in the yard. Mary and Eamonn were having a fight about ownership of a big box of chocolates Joe had left. Suddenly he knew he had made the wrong decision last night: perhaps there was still time.

He ran out the back door and along the Strand Road, turned in to the docks at the Lough Swilly Railway and sped along the quay. He wasn't sure where the Moville tender would be berthed, but he searched every inch of the docks for her. By the time he reached the Guildhall he knew it was no good, but he still walked on as far as the bridge. On his dejected way back he scanned the river, looking down towards the curve of Rosses Bay, but there was no boat there. She was probably steaming past Lisahally by now, or even coming alongside the liner at Moville. It was time to go back, but he didn't want to go.

The memory of that sadness came back to him clearly now, as Eamonn and himself neared Barry Street. He left his brother at the back door and went up the lane to see Nick. He loved looking at the pigeons and would often help with the cleaning-out of their boxes. One of the messenger pigeons landed on the wall now and he wondered about coaxing it into its box. He had done it before, but only when Nick was beside him.

He was pretty sure the pigeon recognised him. You'd know the way it kept cocking its green head from side to side, as it fixed him with a beady eye. He liked its little beak, ever so slightly hooked, and its yellow legs. Nick came quietly out of the kitchen and spoke softly to the bird as he approached it. He took a few corn grains from his pocket and put them on the wall beside her, still talking. The pigeon ruffled up every feather, so that her smooth light-brown chest puffed into a new outline. She stretched, shook herself and started to eat.

'Come over her slowly and put your hand on her,' Nick said. He kept talking to the bird as Sean's hand closed on her. Nick put out more corn and she started to gobble again.

'Lift her slowly now, Sean.'

'The quay is shut, Nick. Did you know that?'

'Aye.'

'I tried to go in and get corn for your pigeons, but the dock-horney put us out. What are you goin' to do now for corn?'

'Would you like a pigeon, Sean?'

'Me? A pigeon?' He felt the old excitement in him again, but knew his mother wouldn't give him the money. She had been very definite about that last time, when he was looking for a half-a-crown to buy one from a friend of Danny's. It hadn't been half as good as Nick's lovely bird, with its white collar and beautiful fan tail that opened out when it flew.

'How much is it, Nick?' He was nearly afraid to put the question.

'I'll let you have it for three-and-six, but you don't have to give me any money now. You can pay me a bit every week out of your pocket money.'

'OK,' Sean said, 'I'll take her.' He didn't want Nick to know that they didn't get regular pocket-money in his house.

'There's an oul box there and it only needs a bit of nettin' wire nailed on to the front. You can have it if you want.'

They walked down the lane, Sean in front with the pigeon hidden under his coat and Nick carrying the wooden box. Sean peeped in through the latch of the back door to make sure his mother was not in the kitchen. They walked quickly into the yard, pulled the bolt of the coalhouse door and entered the pigeon's new home.

'Is that you, Sean?' His mother's voice came to them from the scullery. That meant only a wall separated her from them: they'd have to work quietly if he was to keep his secret.

'Would you chop some sticks there, like a good boy?'

'I'll do it now,' he lied, as they lifted the box containing the bird and placed it on the shelf behind the pile of coal. The pigeon fluttered excitedly, but settled again on its little perch. He knew it was happy enough in its new place when it let itself down until its brown body completely covered the perch, with no yellow legs visible beneath.

He had his own bird at last, but there were problems. It would have to stay ten days in the coalhouse until that dark place became established in its mind as the home to which it would always return. He hoped the proximity of Nick's house wouldn't confuse his bird. He thought of trimming its tail, so that it couldn't fly for a few weeks, but what was the point of that, if the poor bird had to be kept hidden in the coalhouse anyway.

He chopped sticks and put a box full of them in under the stairs, so that his mother wouldn't have to go looking in the coalhouse. She seemed surprised when he told her about the sticks and showed her the bucket filled with coal. He peeped into the coalhouse again, just to be sure the pigeon had settled after the fright he had given her when he shovelled the coal. He put his finger in through the netting-wire and touched her, stroking the black and white interlacing feathers of her tail.

'Where'd you get the bird?'

Eamonn had entered without a sound, startling Sean.

'What do you want in here?' he asked his young brother.

'Jamjars for tadpoles,' Eamonn said, still looking at the pigeon. 'Mammy'll never let you keep her.'

'She's not goin' to know and don't you try tellin' 'er. Do you hear me?'

Eamonn was quick to capitalise on weakness: 'OK, if you come over with me to the Rock field and help us to get tadpoles.

There's millions in the pond, millions.'

Sean was loath to leave the coalhouse, even for half an hour. He thought about tying the bolt, but decided against it. That would only make his mother suspicious.

The pond was away down in the lowest corner of the Rock field. They could see Fred and Roy dipping jamjars into it, as they climbed warily over the barbed wire that separated the Rock field from the far field. They weren't supposed to go in there, but it was only when the apples were ripening in the Rock orchard that the field was well guarded.

Sean gave Eamonn the big two-pound jamjar to hold and went searching for tadpoles with the small one. He didn't like the sliminess of the stagnant pool, nor the green stuff that spread on its surface. He pushed it aside and dipped the jamjar deep. The water froze his arm and he pulled quickly towards the surface. He held the jar up to the light and was happy to see a little black tadpole flicking and zig-zagging its way through the murky liquid.

'Got one,' he shouted across to Eamonn. His brother ran over to examine it, as the water in the jar cleared slowly.

'Put some water in the big jar, Eamonn, and we'll throw him in there.'

'Careful you don't hurt him, Sean.'

'Don't be silly, man: you can't hurt fish.'

'You think you know everything about fish,' Eamonn complained. 'You'll be tellin' us next they like havin' hooks stuck in them.'

That made Sean think of the Faughan and the splashing fish that had avoided their hooks all day. Tadpoles were a lot easier, he thought, as they walked home with their big jamjar full of the little darting creatures. They put them on the scullery window-sill, beside his mother's scrubbing brush.

He had no need to open the coalhouse door, for he could hear the contented cooing of the pigeon – his very own bird.

Chapter Ten

It was Eamonn who first suggested letting the pigeon out of his box, to fly around the coalhouse. Sean wondered why he hadn't thought of it himself: it was such a good idea. He was glad now that his mother had never allowed them to have a dog or cat about the place: having to keep another animal away from his bird now would have complicated the problem.

After its days of confinement, the pigeon at first seemed doubtful about availing of its new freedom. It sat hunched in a corner of the box and defied their best attempts at coaxing. Only when Sean tilted the box up to quite a sharp angle did it emerge in a wild flutter of wings, to find a new vantage point on the top shelf of the coalhouse. At least it can still fly, thought Sean with relief.

He opened the coalhouse door a very little more to let in the air: it brought a welcome brightness into the stuffy darkness and he could see the little motes of coal-dust drifting in the narrow shaft of light from the door.

Eamonn asked him what name he intended to give the bird and he said he hadn't thought about it. In fact, he had given it a lot of thought, He was sure that putting a name on a wild, free creature like a bird was making it even more of a prisoner. He found that a hard thing to explain to himself, which was probably why he didn't even try to make his young brother understand it.

He pulled the door completely closed and they could see nothing in the unexpected darkness.

'Hi! What are you doin', Sean?' Eamonn shouted urgently. 'Open that again.'

'I just wanted to find out what it was like for the pigeon – having the door shut on it.'

'Well, open it till I get out.' Eamonn's voice quivered just a little. 'I'm not goin' to stay here in the dark.'

Eamonn had nailed staples to the inside of the door and the lintel, so that he could hook a little chain between them, allowing about two inches of light to come into the coalhouse. They were sure the bird had brightened up since the little bit of sunlight had entered its life again.

'Imagine,' said Sean, 'only three more days before we can let her out. She's been there a full week now. Could you credit that?'

It had been a week full of deception, of course, trying to hide the existence of the bird from their mother, but on the eighth day the game was up.

'Why aren't youse over in the Crescent playin' these days?' she asked, from the door of the scullery. 'I'm goin' to find out what you're doin' in that oul coalhouse all the time.' She went towards the door but Eamonn prevented her from opening it.

'I'll have to see where she is,' he said, peeping in through the slit to see if it was safe to open the door.

'She! Who's she?' his mother asked.

'She has no name yet,' Eamonn told her solemnly, as he went in, pulling the door after him.

Sean saw straightaway that there was no longer any point in concealment. 'It's a pigeon I got from Nick and we're keepin' her in the coalhouse.'

'A pigeon? Didn't I tell you before there'd be no pigeons in this house. Them birds bring disease wherever they go.'

Eamonn came out of the coalhouse, leaving the door open behind him.

'Would you look at the mess that place is in!'

It was the first time he had noticed that all the coal, and the floor too, was covered with bird-droppings.

'That dirty thing'll have to go,' his mother said with finality. The 'dirty thing' cocked its head and fixed them with an unflinching stare.

His mother would not listen to what they had to tell her about training the bird and about the fact that there were only two days left before that job would be complete. Aunt Cassie came in by the back door and was immediately recruited to the ranks of the opposition. She wouldn't have such things near her house either: everybody knew they were carriers of disease.

Sean wanted to point out to her that Nick's back door was just opposite her own and that the Gallans didn't seem to be suffering from any awful disease, but he knew that it would be a waste of time.

'You'll have to get rid of it before youse go to Drum,' she said. It was the first Sean had heard of going to his Aunt Maggie's.

He turned to his mother: 'When are we goin'?' he asked suspiciously.

'I was thinkin' of next week, but … No! We'll go tomorrow, so you'll have to get rid of that thing immediately. And clean out the mess in that coalhouse too.'

By teatime that evening there was still no change in their situation, though Eamonn and himself knew that it was now only a matter of time.

'When will you give it back to Nick?' Eamonn asked him.

He walked into the coalhouse, pulling the door shut behind him. The pigeon cooed in the darkness. Eamonn was right, of course. It was the obvious thing to do, but he knew he couldn't do it.

He pushed open the door again and the light flooded in. When he pulled the netting wire away from the box, the pigeon was off in a controlled whirring of wings, out over Eamonn's shoulder and rising above the garden wall. He ran out to the yard and they both watched the bird's strong wings powering it upwards, further and further away from the coalhouse.

'What did you let it go for?' Eamonn asked. Sean smiled and then pointed to the bird-droppings: 'Get a scrubbing brush and wash up that place. Move the coal around a bit, so that it won't look so dirty and I'll see to the rest. Let's get this place cleaned up.'

He took the box down from the shelf, lifted the hatchet and began the slow job of turning the pigeon's home into more firewood for his mother.

Mr McAdoo called for them next day in his car. He was one of a small number of car-owners who had been allowed to keep their vehicles after war was declared. The Government seemed to be aware of the important contribution he was making to the war-effort by repairing shoes in Rossville Street. Sean used to wave to him every day on his way to and from school and Mr McAdoo would look out at him over his half-spectacles, give the barest smile and then continue hammering a shoe into his apron, a potato-bag tied around his waist. The Government had given his efforts their seal of approval and Mr McAdoo fully appreciated his importance in society, as he drove the twenty miles to Derry every morning and the twenty miles back to Drum every night. Only Government Forces, and perhaps doctors, were more keenly aware of their status than Mr McAdoo.

He said yes, he'd have a cup of tea if it was in the pot. Sean noticed that he cut open his mother's queen-cakes and filled them with butter and raspberry jam. It was the sort of thing you would do with scones. His mother always said good cakes didn't need anything else.

The car was shining bright at the front door. It had a little gauge sticking up on the bonnet to tell them when the engine was getting hot. Mr McAdoo got a jug of water from his mother and Sean watched him pouring it into the engine. He took a crank-handle from inside the car, inserted it in a hole in the radiator and gave it a turn. He showed Sean how he wrapped his thumb around the handle, alongside his fingers, in case the engine would backfire and break the thumb. Sean kept a knob pulled out on the dashboard for him, until the engine sparked into life.

'Keep it out, keep it out,' Mr McAdoo shouted, as he reached over it himself and clambered into the driving seat.

'Sit in here, Mrs Kane,' he said, patting the seat beside him.

Brid sat behind them, looking after the weans, one on each side of her. Sean and Jenny were thrilled to be in the open air seat, which stuck out at the rear of the car. They could hear Mrs Smith's comments as they pulled away, waving to her and to some of the neighbours who had collected at doors to watch them. A car, right up to your own front door, was a big thing these times.

'I hope they'll be alright,' Mrs Smith said, 'for that car is gie full for such a long trip. It better be a good machine, if it's goin' to make it as far as Dungiven.'

They stopped twice on the way, when the little needle on the bonnet pointed to red. Mr McAdoo got out each time and opened the bonnet, 'to let the air get at her insides'. His mother insisted on them all getting out to empty their bladders, 'just in case'. It was really the weans she was worried about, in case there would be an 'accident' in the back seat; nevertheless, she instructed Brid and Jenny to go through the ritual as well. They objected that they were too old to be peeing on the side of the road, with people passing who might know them, but she had no sympathy.

'Shut your eyes,' she said, 'and nobody will see you.' He knew they were nearing the end of their journey when he saw his mother, in the front seat, pointing out various places to Mr McAdoo and talking animatedly. He couldn't hear her, because of the noise of rushing wind past his ears as their driver headed quickly for Drum. He thought his mother was probably telling Mr McAdoo about all the times they had gone to dances in the area when she was young. He could nearly always tell what she was talking about just by looking at her.

Mr McAdoo sounded the horn three times as they drove into the farmyard, scattering the hens. He stopped in front of the window of the two-storey house and pulled ostentatiously on the ratchet handbrake. His mother made to open the passenger door to get out but he restrained her.

'Don't be in any rush now,' he said calmly. 'Just wait till Maggie comes out to you. It'll give her a minute to get squared up.'

Out she came then, drying her hands on her apron and her face bright with welcome.

'Boys a dear,' she said, 'I never saw youse lookin' better.

Them children is growin' like benweeds. They'll be bigger nor yoursel' soon, Bridie.'

She kissed his mother and shook hands with them. Sean liked the way she used her two hands in doing it and looked directly into his eyes.

'And how is Sean the scholar?' She laughed as she asked: it was her pet name for him.

'I was just bakin' a wheen o' scones for the tay,' she said, turning to Mr McAdoo. 'Come in for a cup, Ian, before you go down home. She'll hardly die for the want of you for a wee while.'

'That's just what I'll not do Maggie, thank you all the same; for she'd be hard to thole if she ever found out I was eatin' scones in Drum while she was heatin' my slippers by our own fireside in Gortnaghey.'

Sean's cousin Mary was taking the last scones from the griddle as they went into the kitchen. She cleaned the flour off it with a home-made brush of stiff feathers and swung it out, away from the fire. Aunt Maggie helped her to unhook it from the chain and put a big black kettle in its place for the tea.

Aunt Maggie was a good bit older than his mother and had spent her married life working, either inside the house, rearing her children, or out toiling on her own small patch, when she wasn't earning a few extra shillings by labouring for neighbouring farmers. She was always on the look-out for needy cases she could help, though there weren't many needier than herself, since the time her husband had emigrated to America. He sent a few letters but never returned. The children stopped asking about their father and Maggie got used to life without a man. She pretended not to care.

She put her freshly-made scones on the table now and a big pot of tea. Sean took his in a bowl rather than in a cup, just to see if he could still drink it the way that he had learned last year. He didn't like the strong taste of the country butter, with the droplets of water still clinging to it.

'You dunno what's good for you,' said his Aunt Maggie, when he told her. She took a packet of margarine from the cupboard, cut a large slice from it and put in on a saucer in front of him.

'We don't eat margarine in our house,' Sean told her.

'You cheeky little skitter,' she said, pretending to be angry. 'You're a chip off the old block and your mother will never be dead as long as you're livin'. That's for sure.'

They all sat around the fire as darkness came. Aunt Maggie lit the big lamp and hung it on the wall. They said the rosary then, hunched over their chairs and kneeling on the uncomfortable concrete floor. He noticed they all had their backsides towards the fire. Aunt Maggie lit a candle and showed himself and Eamonn to their big soft bed up under the roof. It was warm and cosy there, after the sunny day.

Eamonn slept on the inside, under the sloping roof and Sean obeyed his Aunt's instructions to stay on the outside, so that his young brother wouldn't get out of the bed and maybe fall down the stairs.

He seemed to have hardly dropped off to sleep when Eamonn's voice wakened him, calling his name. His brother was not in the bed – he searched every inch of it quickly in the darkness. He felt cold and realised there were no bedclothes on him.

'Where are you, Eamonn?' he called out and was almost afraid to hear the answer.

'Here.' The voice came to him from floor-level, at a distance. His brother had rolled out of bed, taking all the clothes with him and was stuck between the slope of the roof and the side of the bed, unable to move. When Sean finally extricated him and settled the clothes around the both of them, he realised that Eamonn was still confused and hardly awake.

'Where are we, Sean?' he asked timidly.

'You're in your Aunt Maggie's,' said Sean, putting his arm around him, 'and we're goin' to have a great time tomorrow and the day after and the day after…'

Chapter Eleven

The very first thing Sean heard next morning was the crowning of the rooster below them in the yard. The second thing was the sound of his aunt raking the turf fire in the kitchen, to recover the glowing embers from the ashes and blow them into life again. He could still clearly remember the pain he got in his head last year, helping her to blow the first under the first kettle of the day.

He liked being up early and helping his aunt with the jobs, but it was fine to stay in bed this first morning and identify everything by its sound. The rattle of buckets told him that she was preparing food for the hens and he could imagine her strong hands squashing potatoes left over from yesterday's dinner and mixing them with meal. He heard the door opening and the clamour of the hungry chickens increased.

He could see her from the window, carrying two buckets and pushing her way through the birds milling at her feet.

'Birdy, birdy, birdy.' At the sound of her litany, old hens and young chickens came, half running and half flying, over hedges and out of the byre and henhouses. She threw the food in handfuls, spreading it in a circle of neat piles all around her and then moved to a new station with the second bucketful. He saw her throwing a special handful to a weak bird that couldn't fight for its rights. One hen had flown on to the bucket and balanced there, until she pushed it away when she dipped in to gather up the very last of the food. She cleaned the meal from her hands as well, rubbing down each finger individually, so that nothing would be wasted.

Even before his aunt came back into the house, Sean could hear the steady thudding from below. That was probably his cousin Mary churning. She was the early riser and a bit like his aunt. He'd have to get used to country butter again.

He got up quickly and dressed. At the bottom of the stairs, in the little porch, his cousin Betty was preparing the calves' feed.

'Here, Sean: give us a hand wi' this,' she said. 'Pour in the skimmed milk up to there, in them three buckets.' She indicated a point less than half-way up. 'Mix a handful of that meal in with it as well.'

He did as he was told and then followed her out, carrying a single bucket. She had the other two.

'Soog, soog, soog,' she shouted, as they approached the gate of the field. Three calves came running.

'Stand behind me, Sean, till I get the first two right.'

Two calves fought to get their heads into the one bucket and Betty shouted at them not to spill it on her.

'Bring us that other bucket, Sean. Quick.'

The third calf pushed its head in and nearly took the bucket out of his hand. As it sucked contentedly, he could see the tiny white points of new horns coming through its hard head. The sucking became louder and faster as it neared the bottom. He pulled the bucket away when Betty told him to and squeezed out through the narrow opening at the gate. He held it open as she backed out, trying to take the buckets away from the slavering mouths of the calves.

'Right, Sean,' she shouted and he banged it shut.

It was like that every morning of their holiday. One day his aunt asked him to help her collect the eggs. He enjoyed moving the hen in her nest and carefully lifting out the warm brown egg. The basin was nearly full of them, but Aunt Maggie still wasn't satisfied.

'There's a couple of them layin' out and I'm goin' to find where they're layin', if it's the last thing I do.'

They went down the lane, searching the hedges, until they chanced on a cosy little nest with three eggs in it. Sean would never have found it by himself, as it was so well camouflaged. His aunt was elated.

'Didn't I tell you,' she said. 'They'll not get the better of me.'

They were searching the corner of the big back garden when a rooster jumped on one of the hens, flapping furiously.

'What do you keep a rooster for, Aunt Maggie, when it doesn't lay eggs?'

'It would be a gie funny farmyard without one,' she said laughing.

'Sure all he does is screech his head off in the mornin' early and fight with the hens durin' the day.' Sean pointed to the rooster, which had just released the hen.

'I think you'll find she's not complainin'.' His aunt looked directly at him. 'She's his wife, don't you know. Sure there'd be no chickens if the two of them didn't get together now and then. It's the same wi' men and women.'

Sean pondered that for a minute and was about to ask another question, but changed his mind.

Summer had turned into autumn and they were still in Drum. The raspberries had come and gone on the hedges and blackberries which had been green when Mr McAdoo brought the Kanes in his car from Derry had long since turned red and were now deepening into a lovely, rich blackness.

Colgan's shop in Derrylane was offering three-and-sixpence a stone for them and Sean was determined to get rich as quickly as he could. He scratched his arms on the briars as he stretched and stooped to fill his small can before emptying it into the big one that he and his cousin Mary were intent on filling. His fingers bore the purple stain of the fruit.

'I see you're eatin' more than you're pickin',' she said, looking at his mouth.

'Well, nobody's stoppin' you eatin' the odd one either,' Sean said.

'The odd one – how are ye!' exclaimed Mary. 'I wouldn't thank you for them anyway.'

They showed Aunt Maggie the big can filled to the brim with blackberries. She lifted it a few times with her eyes closed, testing its weight.

'There's a stone there anyway, if there's an ounce,' she declared knowledgeably.

When they were crossing the burn, on their way over to Derrylane, Mary put down the can and started to ladle water into it with her hands.

'What are you at?' Sean asked her.

'It'll lend the blackberries a wee bit o' weight,' she said and gave one of Aunt Maggie's laughs.

When they reached Derrylane, Susan Colgan up-ended their can and read the scale of her weighing machine. 'Four shillings, even,' she said, emptying the blackberries into a barrel.

They were a bit more generous with the water on the second day and increased their earnings to four shillings and threepence.

'Boys a dear,' his aunt said when they told her, 'that's power-ful money for blackberries. I've been sweatin' out there in the field all day, tyin' your man's corn, an' I'm sure the oul bugger'll not gimme ten bob for it.' His aunt had a way with words that his mother didn't recommend.

'Did you see the wee rabbit my Mammy brought in the night?' Betty led him over to a shoebox containing something small and brown. He put his hand in and felt the smoothest, warmest fur that he had ever touched. The little animal jerked in fright.

'Where did you find it, Auntie?' he asked.

'It was in the corn,' she said. 'The reaper was makin' smaller and smaller circles around the last bit of the crop and dogs were waitin', all excited, for they had the scent. The mother broke out suddenly to try and lure them away from the young rabbits, but she didn't get ten yards. You should have heard the terrible screechin'. There was only that one little rabbit left when we got the dogs away.'

'Can I keep her, Auntie?' Sean pleaded. 'Please.'

'She can't live without the mother and she's still blind,' his mother said. 'It would be far kinder to kill her.'

He filled a saucer with milk and put it in front of the little animal. Its nose twitched, but it wouldn't touch the milk. He put his finger into the saucer and then held it up to her mouth. A tin-gle ran through his hand and up his arm as the tiny tongue licked the milk from his finger.

'She's mine and I'm goin' to mind her until she grows up.' He didn't look at his aunt or his mother as he spoke, but mar-velled at all the bones moving so delicately under the skin of the rabbit's small head as it sucked the milk. He wondered what its eyes would be like. Probably brown, he thought.

As they went upstairs to bed he heard his mother saying, 'He gets too attached.' He knew they were talking about him.

Betty fed the calves by herself next morning. Sean needed all his time for feeding the rabbit, which kept licking his finger as long as there was milk there. His cousin Mary had finished her work and was shouting at him to come on for the blackberries. It was their last day and they were determined to make it the most productive yet. He thought about the rabbit: it would have to stay inside Mr McAdoo's car on the way back to Derry – it would be far too windy for it in the open seat at the back. Brid would be happy enough to swap seats with him.

They could hear the whirring of the reaper in the last field of their neighbour's corn. It was all coming to an end together – corn and blackberries and holidays. He would put his jersey around the rabbit in her box to keep her warm on the way home.

The can was full of blackberries again. They went down the lane towards the burn, but Mary stopped before they reached it. A spout stuck out from the ditch and spring-water was cascading from it.

We'll fill it up here,' Mary said, 'and we'll make it the full five bob on your last day.'

'That's no right,' Sean protested, 'and anyway, she'll know for certain.'

'Divil the know,' Mary laughed. 'Sure isn't it far easier sellin' water than sellin' blackberries?'

Susan was shutting the shop as they arrived, hot and out of breath.

'Man dear,' she said, lifting the heavy can and emptying its contents on to the scales, 'that can is still growin'.' She scrutinised the scales. 'It's five shillings and a penny this time.'

'Ah! Just make it the even five bob,' Mary said generously.

'Alright so,' Susan said, 'but I'd better give you some of it back, in that case.'

She lifted the big bowl full of blackberries from the scales and inclined it slightly over the can. The black 'juice' ran out and tumbled noisily into the empty can.

Susan looked at them for a good while before she spoke.

'Well, youse had a grand time wi' the blackberries,' she said. 'You'll hardly be doin' any more pickin' yoursel', Mary, now that your cousin is goin' back to Derry.'

On the way back along the lane, Sean felt a terrible guilt about selling all that water to Susan, but Mary told him not to worry about it.

'What are you girnin' about, man?' she asked. 'Didn't we get the five bob?'

Everybody was busy cleaning up the house when they got back to Aunt Maggie's. They were going to have a big night for the end of the harvest. There was a shiny accordion on the settle bed in the lower room. Aunt Maggie told him that its owner, 'Simey' McCloskey, was a powerful man for the music. Sean tried a few notes on the keyboard, pulling the bellows with his other hand. *O'Donnell Abu* sounded better on it than on his Aunt Cassie's piano. His mother had made an enormous pile of soda farls and was starting a batch of wheaten bread. She looked hot and flustered. Brid was brushing the dust of the kitchen floor into the fireplace.

'Go easy with that brush,' her mother said, 'or you'll ruin the bread.'

'Hi, Brid,' Sean called to her from the other room, 'how

about swappin' seats in the car tomorrow, so that I can have the rabbit beside me.'

'There's no rabbit goin' to Derry,' his mother said firmly, blowing a strand of hair out of her face as she lifted the bread.

'Well, I'm not goin' either then.' Sean was determined to win the struggle this time.

He was put to bed early for his stubbornness, without any supper. The hunger was bad enough, but missing the music was far worse. The only consolation was that he had managed to sneak the rabbit upstairs with him, when his mother wasn't looking. He put the box on the floor beside the bed and stretched down his hand to touch its smooth fur. He could feel its tiny heart pulsing.

The accordion woke him and the sound of singing: '... and we'll wave the green flag wildly over the hills of Glenswilly.' He recognised his aunt's voice. She was a good singer.

He must have dozed off again and was awakened by a man's voice, calling for the 'Lancers'. The accordion played a fast tune to the accompaniment of battering feet. There was the clinking of cups then and the voice of his mother singing 'As I walked out on a May mornin', near the verdant braes of Screen, I put my back to a mossy bank...' That was all Sean heard before he dropped off to sleep again, his outstretched hand touching the rabbit.

It was gone when he woke next morning: not even the box was there by his bed. He heard his aunt moving downstairs and he ran down to her, rubbing the sleep from his eyes. She was clearing up after the big night.

'Who took my rabbit?'

'Is it gone?' she said. 'It was the cat took it.'

He saw his jersey on the sofa – the one that he had put around the rabbit last night to keep it warm. He went down to the lower room to search for it. The accordion lay on the bed again, but he didn't try to play it this time. He looked under the bed, just in case his rabbit had escaped, but there was only fluff and dust there and old shoes.

None of them seemed surprised when Aunt Maggie told them that his rabbit had been taken by a cat. He wondered about a cat carrying a big cardboard shoebox.

He sat with Jenny in the open back-seat of Mr McAdoo's car on the way home, but the excitement of the earlier journey was gone. He kept thinking about his lovely rabbit and prayed that it still had life somewhere – that it would yet get the chance to open its blind eyes and see the world.

When they reached Barry Street, Sean went out into the back yard to find that the tadpoles they had caught in the Rock field before the holidays were transformed. They had lost their tails and some were growing legs. The more senior members had become frogs, hopping around the garden.

'Would you look at my lovely frogs,' Eamonn said excitedly.

'Aye, they're gorgeous,' answered Sean, 'but they can't stay here. You'll have to put them back in the pond.'

Chapter Twelve

Meadowbank Avenue never quite recovered its respectability after they came with oxy-acetylene burners to strip its iron gates and railings. Sean heard that the iron was needed in the war against Hitler, but other people said it was being stacked in enormous useless piles up in Rosemount and that the whole affair was one big act of bluff.

Meadowbank's little front gardens were now open to marauding children, either looking for lost footballs or daring each other to trespass in what had been virgin territory in the days of railings, when squeaky iron gates would give loud warning of invaders. There was nothing like that any more and trespassing in an open garden did not have the thrill of scaling pointed railings with all its attendant dangers. In Sean's eyes Meadowbank had lost face: you couldn't have the same respect for an avenue that had only little stumps of iron where graceful railings used to be.

Most of the Protestant residents bid farewell to their railings with a good grace and hoped it would be the Meadowbank railings that would win the war: it was the same for the majority of the Catholic minority, for they had begun to think like good 'Prods', after years of continuous striving towards the respectability of their neighbours. The bottom end of the Avenue wasn't quite as respectable as the top and the oxy-acetylene burners were not at all so loyally welcomed there, in either Protestant or Catholic homes.

Protestants didn't keep greyhounds. Everybody knew that, but Sean wondered why. Only two houses in Barry Street had them and walked them regularly. The owners were Catholics, of course, and Sean regarded the dogs as Catholic too: there had never been a Protestant greyhound in Derry. He began to wonder what the other greyhounds in the traps in the Brandywell would do if they sensed a Protestant dog, ready to race.

A bookie had recently opened his shop at the bottom of Barry Street, in a small room at the side of Joe's fish and chip saloon. Sean couldn't really know what it was like inside, from the hurried glances he gave as he passed. His mother waged continuous and holy war against such Catholic vices. She was right about it being a Catholic sin, he thought: you'd know to look at them that all the fellows hanging around the door of the bookie's shop were 'Fenians', though he had heard tell that their neighbour, Hugh Peart, sometimes visited there. They said his mother had been a Catholic, but nobody talked much about that sort of thing. He was reminded of the day his mother had been talking to their Protestant neighbour, Mrs Smith, about the poor Stewarts. 'And the daughter married a Catholic – could anything be worse than that?' asked Mrs Smith. It was only in such unguarded moments that the veils were lifted.

His mother said Catholics didn't need to be trying to win a fortune on the dogs or horses anymore, as there were now plenty of good jobs since the war had started. She didn't mention the other Catholic vices of billiards, cards and pitch-and-toss, but Sean knew they were included there somewhere, for she usually lumped them all together. Most of the Protestants Sean knew were pretty well off and regarded their neighbours' vices as being due to thriftlessness or even to Catholicism itself. But the real-life odds for a Catholic in Derry were miserable. A pound on the dogs was always a better bet.

There was work available now alright: evidence of it was in the big blockades that were being erected down the Strand Road, near the level-crossing, where the Lough Swilly train stopped the traffic on its way to Fahan and Buncrana. The blockades were made of concrete and were positioned so as to slow down or completely stop enemy tanks. Derry people wondered if it was the Germans or the Irish they were worried about, since the Strand Road led directly to the 'Free State', either via Buncrana or Moville. Whoever the enemy might be, the Derry citizens of Messines Park and Shantallow were clearly expendable, since they had been left outside the fortifications in these new contingency plans for the second glorious siege of Derry! Sean's only serious objection to the blockades was that they forced him to steer his bicycle at a narrow angle across the railway lines, when he tried the new route. His front wheel slipped into the track and he came off in a hurry, not at all impressed by the new fortifications.

On waste ground between the blockades and the Foyle, enormous temporary buildings were springing up. A large party of flamboyant American technicians had arrived to prepare the way for their troops. One couldn't help noticing the bright clothes they wore, even at work. Sean was sure that Derry people did buy new clothes now and again, since shops up the town were selling them, but Derry dress was not bright and it never seemed to change: you'd always recognise people at a distance by what they wore. The American technicians changed the fashion-face of the city and increased the pace of its life. For them, speed was everything.

A Derry man whom they had employed to help in the work was doing his best to loosen a tight nut. It was his first job in some twenty years of signing the dole. The 'Yank' looked at his struggles for a few moments before he spoke.

'Hi, buddy,' he said, in a not unfriendly voice, 'shit or get off the pot.'

Life was never the same again after the American Forces landed in Derry. The town was jammed with lorries and jeeps full of happy people. They did not have the heavy boots and clicking heels of the English 'Tommies', but were more relaxed and friendly: they certainly made much closer contact with the people of Derry – particularly the girls.

It wasn't that Derry girls had disliked the seduction style of the English Tommies, but most of them found the American technique irresistible: it included unheard-of delicacies like mouth-watering Hershey's chocolate, so different from the dark brown wartime chocolate they were used to. Cigarettes came in new exciting packets and whole cartons of them could suddenly appear if the job was right. The 'Camel' was more potent than the 'Player'.

As if that were not enough to seduce the 'Maiden City', the Yanks hit poor Derry with their chewing gum. Sean and his friends scrambled for it and for coins and sweets thrown to them from passing jeeps. They had no defence against succulent American confectionery, after the tastelessness of wartime rationed sweets and chewing-gum that became bland rubber after a dozen chews. Who would blame Derry girls for succumbing to their other awful temptations? What hope had virtue against the novelty of nylons?

Even the holy nuns of St Eugene's fell under their spell: the

Yanks organised a big party for the girls' classes and the nuns responded by teaching the students to sing the *Star-Spangled Banner.* Sean learned it by listening to Brid and Jenny.

'Then conquer we must, when our cause it is just and this be our motto – in God is our trust.'

To have the 'conquered' singing those lines with swelling hearts and feeling like conquerors themselves was no bad trick.

Sean envied his sisters the good things the Americans gave them to eat. Above all else, he desired the luscious Californian apples with the shiny red skins – the sort they had not seen in Derry since war had been declared – and that was becoming a long time ago, he thought.

Mary brought one of the apples home from the party and left it on the mantelpiece. For her it was just another apple: she was too young to remember what the American apples were like before the war – sitting in their wooden boxes in the shops, all individually wrapped in white tissue paper. He asked her for it but she refused him, giving it to Eamonn instead, as they went upstairs together: being a wean meant going to bed earlier than everybody else.

Later that evening his mother cut short the rosary, omitting all the trimmings at the end. He was still thinking of the red apple when she sent him upstairs: 'Say all your own wee prayers in bed – and no readin', mind.'

Praying in bed was acceptable, but reading in bed was a sin which his mother was determined to eliminate. It was a continuous struggle between them. If Sean heard her coming up the stairs he'd hop out of bed to switch off the light and be back in, pretending sleep, when she'd open the door. She had caught him once or twice by gong out to the back yard and looking up to see the light in the window. Eamonn and he shared a single bed in the small room above the coalhouse and toilet. They called it the 'back return' and it was separated from the other two bedrooms by a short flight of stairs. The threat of the light being spotted from the back yard made Sean decide to live less dangerously than before and only put on the light to read after his mother had gone up the stairs to her own room and had shut the door. Even this precaution had recently proved insufficient, for she had come out of her room again one night and spied the light coming from under the door of the 'back-return'. When she came into the room, his eyes were shut in angelic sleep, but he didn't think he had really convinced her.

That was why he was now putting coats and trousers behind the door, as a first step in the inauguration of the most sophisticated anti-mother equipment yet devised. As he started to undress he saw the stump of Eamonn's red apple in the fireplace. His brother probably didn't even realise what kind of an apple it was – what a pedigree it had. He was sad at the shameful waste.

Eamonn stirred, half-opened his eyes and enquired sleepily, 'What time is it?'

Some badness inside Sean, probably connected with Californian apples, made him say, 'Eight o'clock. Hurry or we'll be late for school.'

Being late for school was a serious matter, so Eamonn made praiseworthy efforts to get up, even though sleep still held him tightly in her grasp. Sean stopped taking off his clothes and started to put them on again. Eamonn tried to do the same thing, but could hardly stand. Sean kept encouraging him to continue, reminding him how late they were for school. He was even kind enough to give Eamonn a hand with the trousers, as the poor fellow kept falling sideways every time he lifted his leg. Only when he was fully dressed did Sean reveal the deception. Eamonn's muttered threats included a certain word that Sean had never heard his young brother use before.

Sean was determined to have a long read tonight. He was already half-way through *Tom Sawyer* and the book had to go back to the class library tomorrow, so he couldn't afford to be caught by his mother tonight. He checked that no chink of light was escaping beneath the door and then took from his pocket the new anti-mother equipment, built to his own design. It was nothing more than two cup-hooks and a length of twine.

He had some difficulty getting the first hook screwed into the door-frame, high up beside the wall and just above the door-opening. Normally he would have started the screw with a few blows of a hammer, but absolute silence was necessary on this job. He made a loop in the end of the twine and hooked it over the old-fashioned brass light switch. Then he checked that he could switch off by pulling up on the string, which he threaded through the first cup-hook. So far, so good.

The second cup-hook proved easier and he soon had it snugly screwed in on the other side of the door frame, high up above his bed. When the string from the switch was threaded through the two hooks, the end of it came nicely to his hand where he lay in bed. He was nearly afraid to try it, in case it didn't work.

He pulled on it and the light went out: he knew he had his mother beaten. No matter how late he'd hear her step on the stairs and he would still have time to pull the switch and pitch the room into darkness. He got out of bed and switched on the light again to give it a final check, then lay in bed with his book in one hand and the dangling end of the string in the other.

He was absorbed in *Tom Sawyer* when he heard his mother ascending the stairs to bed. He was in no hurry, but waited until she was almost at the top of the first flight of stairs before calmly pulling the string. She stopped outside his door and he knew she was waiting for the tell-tale rustle of book-leaves turning. He held his breath until she had started to mount the last few steps to her own room. Only after he had heard her quietly snibbing the door did he get out of bed to switch on again. He was so confident now that he didn't even try to quieten the noisy switch.

As he lay in bed reading he thought about having another string around the bottom of the door, so that he could switch on the light again after interruptions, without having to get out of bed. His invention would just go on and on, getting better and better.

Tom Sawyer was enthralling reading, but Sean's eyes were beginning to close when his mother burst open the door, pushing coats and trousers in front of her and reaching for the light-switch. Sean pulled on the string in panic and knew that he had caught his mother's hand in it. He dropped the book and feigned sleep.

His mother was angry. He had nipped her finger and she had pulled his whole wonderful invention down on her head, frightening herself.

'Don't you lie there pretendin' to be asleep,' she hissed in a loud whisper, so as not to waken Eamonn or the other children, but he feared it more than her biggest shout. 'Just you wait till I get the strap at you in the mornin'. I'll put readin' in bed out your head.'

The prospect of vengeance by both his mother and Eamonn threatened to make tomorrow even worse than today, he thought, as he tried to sleep. Red Californian apples were confused with the memory of Eamonn's sleepy stumblings. A picture of falling off the bicycle at the blockades came into his mind and his cut knees still stung where the bedclothes touched them.

Chapter Thirteen

Before he was fully awake Sean could hear the noise outside his bedroom. It was a kind of shuffling and sliding sound that he couldn't quite recognise and it was confused with his waking dreams. He opened the door and went out on to the landing, clearing sleep from his eyes.

His mother was removing the stair-carpet. He had quite forgotten that this was the day for the annual carpet-beating in the far field.

'Sean, would you lift that carpet off the small stairs and then give us a hand with the one in the parlour?'

He knelt down to free the iron clips that held the carpet on each side, happy that last night's troubles had not been mentioned. He rolled up the carpet and collected the dusty stair-pads.

'We're doin' the carpets the day,' answered Sean. 'We'll bate the linin' outa them.'

'Are we all goin'?' said Eamonn.

'Of course we are, an' we're havin' a picnic. Roll up that bit on the landin' there.'

His voice echoed down into the hall, now that the carpet had been removed: the loud empty sound of his mother's steps on the bare wooden stairs reminded him of last year. The girls were awake by the time they went to remove the carpet in the parlour: they all lifted one side of the piano while Mary slid it out, with warnings from her mother not to forget the under-carpet. The settee and chairs were easy after that.

Carrying the rolled-up parlour carpet over to the field was like supporting a crocodile, Sean thought, as he led the way, with Jenny in the middle and Brid supporting its tail. It was heavy and the rough backing hurt his bare arms. His mother carried the main stair-carpet, while Eamonn brought the small pieces and the stair-pads in a bag. Mary followed them with a selection of sticks and broken brush-handles for the workers. The proper carpet-beater that they used to have, made of twisted cane, was only a memory now.

They unrolled the carpets and turned them face downwards on the grass, having first carefully checked that no donkey or cow had left anything behind on the ground. He knew that his mother would not be too happy at the thought of them battering that sort of thing into her best carpet. The dust rose in a cloud around them, as they laid into it with their sticks. When they tired, Sean and Brid pulled the carpet to a new position for the second round of the battering and the weans marvelled at the thick layer of dust their labours had left on the flattened grass.

They unrolled the stair-carpet then and found they had acquired new carpet-beaters from the Crescent. Fred, Roy and Stanley were poised with sticks at the ready and Sue Mackey had run home to get a brush-handle. Sean had not realised till then how ravelled and torn the stair-carpet was and he felt a little stab of shame in front of the others. Mary sat on the small stair-carpet, holding firmly to the sides of it, while Stanley pulled her nearly the length of the field. He was easily the strongest of them all.

Sean saw his mother coming across the Crescent, carrying a

full shopping bag. They sat down on the parlour carpet and waited for her. She spread the oil-cloth from the kitchen table and brought out sandwiches and a bottle of fizzy lemonade. She had the small flask that Sean took to school every day, filled now with tea for herself and plenty of extra cups for their helpers. He was glad she had thought of that.

'Them's great sandwiches, Mrs Kane,' Stanley said.

Sean felt Stanley should know that best, since he had eaten more of them than anyone else. His mother opened a packet of digestive biscuits and passed them round.

'God, I wish my mother did the carpets out in the field like this,' Stanley said, fervently munching.

Sean's mother asked them about their new schools. Roy was to go to Foyle College on Monday, but Stanley was staying on at the Model School. Sue would be in the girls' High School, up Duncreggan Road. He just couldn't imagine her there, wearing the hat with the striped band around it. Neither could he imagine himself and Fred wearing the blue blazers of St Columb's College. It all made him realise that it was the last day of the holidays, if one didn't count Sunday.

Sean's blazer was a hand-me-down from his cousin Francis, who was away now, studying to be a priest. It had the arms of the College on the pocket and the motto 'Quaerite Primum Regnum Dei'. His mother told him it meant 'seek first the kingdom of God'.

He liked the fuss that his mother made over him, about going to St Columb's. It started with a bath in his Aunt Cassie's house on Sunday night, as well as new underwear and socks that were still joined together at the top. The shoes felt stiff and heavy and his heels slipped up and down in them when he walked. His mother believed in buying 'sensible' shoes with a 'bit of room for growin''. He had always wanted a shoulder-satchel for his schoolbooks, but now that he had one, he was not so sure about it.

He barely recognised Roy on the bus, with his new uniform and the peak of his cap pulled right down over his eyes. You'd never see a Catholic wearing a cap that way, he thought. They had nothing to say to each other and he was glad when Roy got off at Lawrence Hill to go up to Foyle College. He could see him chatting excitedly to another carefully-uniformed student as they went up the hill.

It was strange to pass his usual bus-stop at Great James's Street and remain on the bus to Guildhall Square. He wondered about Danny and Charlie, who had stayed on at the Christians. He was glad that he'd no longer have to pass the terrible smell of the gasworks on Lecky Road every morning. Bishop Street was wider and seemed more interesting in a way, with the Diamond, Derry Walls and the Jail, though you'd miss the wee shops of Rossville Street.

All the new students were assembled in the 'Big Study' and the Dean told them that there would be two days of examinations to decide which classes they would be in. It came as a shock, for Sean had assumed that as a scholarship holder he'd be spared further tests. He was afraid to risk his new fountain-pen in the dirty inkwell on the desk, but filled it from his own big bottle of 'Quink' with the wide bottom. This was a new world, he thought, replacing the bottle carefully in his satchel.

That evening, on the bus home, he took out the pen and looked at the fourteen carat gold nib. He had hardly stopped writing all day and she hadn't let him down once. She didn't feel new and strange any more. He jumped off the bus at the Factory and started to race it to the other end, though the satchel bumping on his back and the new shoes made it difficult. He always raced the bus at examination times. If he was past the last pillar of the Factory before it, he'd be first in the class: if he only got as far as the second-last pillar he'd be second in the class. He beat it comfortably this evening, though he got some help from old Mrs Mullan, who hobbled slowly out of the bus after him. The examinations were easy anyway.

As he came in the bottom lane from Meadowbank, a big man with a country accent asked him where he'd get a pump. Sean started to explain to him where Barber's bicycle-shop was, but the man didn't seem very interested. Instead, he turned down towards the waste ground and started to pee against the wall of the old billiard-room.

His mother plied him with questions about St Columb's and what he had done the first day. The questions were long and his answers short. He wanted to hold on to St Columb's for himself. No, he hadn't been asked about his cousin who was going to be a priest and he hadn't met Fr McGahan, who was a 'far-out friend' of his mother's people. Yes, he had drunk the tea out of the flask and yes, it was still hot and yes, he had kept his blazer on all day. Yes, he had answered all the questions in the examinations and he hadn't forgotten blotting paper and he had plenty left for tomorrow.

He thought it a good time to bring up the question of pocket-money again, but the answer was still 'no'. He found it hard to believe that his new status and responsibilities did not merit regular pocket-money. What was the good of having a College blazer and nothing to put in it? His mother laughed when he told her about the countryman looking for the pump and so did Brid. Sean himself seemed to be the only one who did not understand country language.

When the examinations finished on the second day they were given a choice of school subjects. The selection of Geography rather than History was easy, for he had never done any history at school, whereas he knew all about land masses and the capital cities of nearly every country in the world and the most intimate industrial details of all the towns in Ireland, in a long list beginning with 'Arklow – pottery and fishing'. He would have liked French, but the President, Dr Eugene O'Doherty, gave them a long lecture about the priesthood and how those thinking about going to Maynooth should choose Greek rather than French.

For years now, he had always said he was going to be a priest when he grew up. His mother sometimes talked about him becoming a telegram-boy at fifteen and eventually getting behind the counter in the Post Office. Catholics could get jobs there, since it was a part of the British Imperial Civil Service and wasn't controlled by Protestants, as the Northern Ireland Civil Service was. He'd heard his mother and Aunt Cassie talking about it. But that decision could wait until he was fifteen: the decision about the Church had to be made straight away, so he opted for the Church and chose Greek. Everybody had to do Irish and Latin. He wanted the Irish, but he wasn't so sure about the Latin.

Next day the class lists were posted on the notice-board outside the Big Study. He was distraught at first to find himself in the D class but John Divis, who was in third year, told him that D was the top class and A the weak one. John was from Coleraine and had been a boarder since his first day at St Columb's. He saw Sean as a new exciting source of daily lunches which would supplement his meagre boarders' diet, while Sean was happy to have an experienced guide to his new world.

John brought him down to one of the football pitches where they were playing soccer with a small ball. He had a word with the goalkeeper and they joined in the match, one on each side. It wasn't at all like the football he had played in the far field at home. For one thing, the teams here were enormous – he reckoned there must have been anything up to a hundred fellows of all ages playing. They didn't hold positions as you'd do normally, but followed the ball in droves. He realised he'd have to speed up and pass the ball quickly if he was to survive in this kind of football. He was relieved when the chapel bell rang for the start of afternoon classes.

He did a deal with John for two books, *Everyday Life in Ancient Rome and Everyday Life in Ancient Greece.* He got them for half-a-crown and knew his mother would be pleased. It had come as a surprise to him that he had already done more Maths than students from other schools. The geometry book he had used in the Christian Brothers was the one recommended here too and they were starting again at the first theorem. It made him feel quite superior. But the fellows from Rosemount school knew far more Irish. They had already used the book *Fios Feasa* and could answer questions in Irish addressed to them by Mr McGonigle. It was a big disappointment for Sean, coming from what was always regarded in Derry as the 'Irish' school. In the Christian Brothers you tended to look down your nose at the 'Irish' efforts of other schools and Sean had got used to being on the winning side in Feis competitions for Irish singing and action songs, without understanding what he was singing about.

He had a clear picture in his mind of an action song they had not won, but which had impressed a packed house in the Guildhall for the wrong reason. It was about haymakers and a duckling: Sean still did not know the story of it, even though he was singing it out in Irish at the top of his voice and following the whispered cues of the Christian Brother. He knew he was a haymaker, for he had a wooden rake in his hand and was dressed in rustic fashion, much of his outfit being of crepe paper.

The haymakers were tightly crowded in the narrow back-entrance to the stage just before the show began and the tension was nearly unbearable. Sean could hear a piano in the distance, playing music that was vaguely familiar, but it was only when the haymaker in front of him disappeared that he realised the show was on. Someone pushed him forward and he saw a thousand Derry faces staring at his awkward efforts to catch up with the rest of the dancing team. They sang and raked until the nervous duckling appeared, wearing white pantaloons and a light-blue jacket with white buttons. He made his way to the front of the stage, the haymakers went silent and the duckling's solo began. It was easy to see that the audience was affected, but it was only afterwards that Brid and Jenny explained to him through their laughter how the duckling had stolen the show. It transpired that the poor bird's nerves and bladder control were somehow connected, with the inevitable result. The audience watched spellbound as the damp circle on his beautiful white pantaloons grew bigger and bigger, with each succeeding verse of his very moving song.

But all the Irish songs learned by rote at the Christian Brothers counted for nothing at St Columb's and yet Sean was determined to occupy this new Irish world. He had as much right to be there as any fellow from Rosemount.

His mother was glad to hear that he had met John Divis. The family had been good friends of hers in Coleraine and Mr Divis had been at sea with Eamonn Kane. Sean knew he'd have no difficulty getting lunches for John. His mother had already told him to invite John down to their house on his first free Saturday.

He wanted to go over the Crescent in his school uniform, but his mother insisted on him changing into his old clothes. He said he'd keep on his uniform for going up the lane to Aunt Cassie's house. Kathleen, his cousin and godmother, was there when he went in. She put half-a-crown into the top pocket of his blazer and Aunt Cassie gave him a big thick Greek Lexicon which had belonged to his cousin Francis. He went out the front door to go home, so that he could look across the Crescent. Roy was in his Foyle College blazer, talking to Sue Mackey in her High School outfit. They seemed closer and friendlier than he had ever seen them before. He was sure they had seen him, but they gave no sign.

Chapter Fourteen

Sean's new Maths teacher was Fr Teehan, but none of the students called him that. Everyone knew him as 'The Bird'. He was well aware of his nickname. He professed to have no interest in literature, but saw the whole world in terms of mathematics. He had the disconcerting habit of swinging round suddenly from his blackboard and throwing chalk at the head of anyone he thought had been talking instead of concentrating on his mathematics lesson. The victim was expected to bring back the chalk and continue the teacher's calculations on the blackboard.

Fr Teehan came into the class one day to find that a student had chalked up on the board: 'Hail to thee blithe spirit, bird thou never wert'.

'Who wrote that?' demanded the 'Bird'.

'Please sir, Shelley,' a voice from the back called.

'Come out here, Shelley,' the 'Bird' said menacingly.

Sean was beginning to acquire a considerable store of poems. Their English teacher, Mr McAuliffe, was a real stickler for poetry learning and always gave them large chunks to learn for the next class. He'd often meet Charlie Stewart going to school and the two of them would go down Bishop Street, reciting furiously to each other, not caring who heard them.

One day a week, Mr McAuliffe's class was devoted to essay reading, as good essays were the love of their teacher's life. A sign of exceptional favour was to have one's essay torn gently out of the copy book, to be put among his prize offerings which stretched back over many years and were kept locked in his desk. He had a less gentle way of tearing other essays out and throwing them into the dustbin, with shouts of 'rubbish – absolute rubbish' and stern commands to rewrite the lot.

Sean enjoyed the relaxation of the class, when he didn't have to read his own essay. Today's victim was Leo Kane from the Waterside and the essay was on 'Flying'. Leo was not one of the best students, but he surprised them all with a passage of high-flowing purple prose about air travel, finishing up with the impressive denouement '…we look at the bird and are humbled'. Leo was showing a literary style that no-one had suspected, but Mr McAuliffe was not impressed.

'You copied this from another essay,' he said.

This was serious stuff. Sean held his breath as the teacher rummaged through his prize essays. He selected one and closed the lid of the desk with a bang. It was on 'Flying' and had been done by a brilliant student some years earlier. It was the very same essay, word for word, right down to 'we look at the bird and are humbled'. When he had finished reading it, the teacher looked out over his glasses at Leo.

'Well, do you own up now? Didn't you copy from this essay?'

'No, sir,' answered Leo and received a cuff on the ear from the angry teacher.

Sean thought it was time for Leo to come clean. Surely he could see that there was no way out. Mr McAuliffe was infuriated by the student's stubbornness.

'How did you break into my desk?' he shouted.

'Please sir, I didn't.'

It earned him another blow and made him decide to confess that he had done exactly what the previous brilliant student had done – copied it word for word from *Encyclopaedia Britannica*.

They had Fr Ruane for Religious Knowledge. He was a big, soft-spoken man and his religion was a gentle persuasive thing. Sean really liked him. One day they had a visit from the Dean, whose religion was of the stern, unbending type. He was in the process of scouring the whole school, hunting out copies of the New Testament which might be a danger to their Catholic faith and morals.

Sean's copy was a Douay version, without an imprimatur, which he had purchased cheaply from an Indian traveller who regularly visited Aunt Maggie's house. He had a big suitcase full of exotic silk clothes and scarves, perched precariously on his bicycle. His Aunt Maggie always protested that she didn't want anything, but the Indian kept soft-talking her, knowing that once he had the case opened before her on the floor, with the goodies spread out, she couldn't resist. Sean had paid him two shillings for the New Testament. He resented the Dean confiscating it now, with dire warnings about using unapproved texts. Sean had never seen the book as a threat to his morals. He began to understand that while the President might be the boss, the Dean had God as an ally.

John Divis met him at lunch time and Sean gave him the sandwiches his mother had prepared.

'I see you're eighth linesman in the football on Saturday,' he said.

Sean had no idea what he meant, but John explained the intricacies of the gaelic football grading system in the College. Eighth linesman was the lowest grade of all, so they weren't expecting much from him. It was just as well, he thought, as he had never before played with a big ball. He'd have to get boots – proper ones with studs – a College jersey and togs. His captain was Joe Ward and he was a prefect as well, so he had double authority. Prefects were in a different world from that of the 'yaps', as the new students were called. Sean didn't know what the word meant, but he was sure it was not complimentary.

His mother was adamant that he couldn't have the money for football boots or togs. He told her about all the expensive cricket gear that Roy had got for Foyle College, but it was no good.

'We just haven't got the money for it,' she said.

But Sean had an idea that if it had been for books or something educational she would have found it. Football was low on her priority list, even gaelic football.

His first game, played in pouring rain, was a disaster. He wore an old pair of boots belonging to John. They were far too big for him and let in water. His hands were so wet and cold that he failed to hold the ball when it came to him. He realised that with his Richmond Crescent background he knew more of the rules of rugby than of this other game, which was supposed to be the Catholic one. The ball came to him suddenly and he surprised himself by holding on to it this time. Joe Ward, standing near him, shouted for it and Sean was happy to throw it to him. The referee's whistle blew and he knew he had made a foul pass. Why did they have to have such finicky rules about a simple thing like passing a ball? It was nearly as bad in the Protestant game of rugby, where you had to throw the ball backwards, even though you would be trying to go forward. He thought he'd forget the religious games and stick to soccer with a small ball.

He had gone over the Crescent at the weekend and watched

them playing cricket. Even that seemed to have changed. It was
all about style and a high elbow and taking cover behind your
pads with your backside in the air. He wondered what had happened to all the sport they used to have: it seemed to have disappeared with the home-made bats and the soft ball. Danny
Guerin, who was at school with him in St Columb's, went in to
bat. They tried to make him change his baseball style of holding
the bat and conform to the proper cricket style of Foyle College.
Roy, who was bowling, asked him if he wanted 'middle and leg'.

'I dunno,' said Danny, 'just you toss them up here and I'll welt
them.'

He bounced the first one off the garage roof and lofted the
second into the Rock field. He soon had the fielders running all
directions to control his vulgar Catholic display of non-cricket.
Sean enjoyed it hugely: it reminded him of the happy times.

The Choirmaster at St Columb's was Mr Maultsaid. He
brought them up to the chapel organ for a singing test and Sean
was selected for the choir. They began to learn 'Ave Verum': it
was a hymn he had always loved. He remembered having seen Mr
Maultsaid conduct the Brass and Reed Temperance Band at the
Long Tower Church last year. They had marched to the church
from the Christian Brothers' School, wearing oak leaves in their
lapels for the feast of St Columba. It was a lovely day and the
sound of the band moved him deeply as it accompanied the
hymn to St Columba:

Saint Columba, holy father,
Hear our praises, grant our prayer.
Help thy children here in Derry:
Thou the Holy Church's dove.

They always had a free day for the feast of St Colmcille, to give him his Irish name. Since it wasn't a holy day of obligation there was no need to go to mass, but he wouldn't have missed the evening service in the grounds of the Long Tower Church for anything. He wondered if he'd get a free day for St Colmcille next time, now that he was in St Columb's, the saint's own college.

The choir practice had gone on until teatime that day, but Sean was well aware that Mr McAuliffe wouldn't accept such an excuse for not having his poetry learned. Next morning he got off the bus at Great James's Street and was already well into *Morte d'Arthur* as he ascended Waterloo Street.

'So all day long the noise of battle rolled ...'

He was past Governor Walker's statue and the Protestant Cathedral when 'Sir Bedevere, the last of all his knights bore him to a chapel nigh the field'.

The poetry seemed to be going into his head well this morning, if he could only hold on to it. As he passed the Labour Exchange, or the 'Brew' as everybody called it, he had double-checked 'the goodliest fellowship of famous knights whereof this world holds record' and decided to leave it at that and hope for the best. There was still Irish grammar to be done and only about four hundred yards between him and the College gates.

All the boarders and some of the day-boys were gathered around the door of the senior-house: he hurried up the walks to see what it was all about. They said the new prefects were up with the President, asking for a free day. With that, the three prefects emerged and gave a thumbs-up sign. The sudden roar of the students scattered the birds from the senior-house roof and day-boys running down Bishop Street for school knew that there was no longer any hurry. Irish irregular verbs and the harrowing tale of King Arthur's death were no longer a heavy load weighing down on Sean's mind and a long day of freedom stretched out before him.

He enjoyed his first retreat at St Columb's. It was a weekend of prayer and recollection, conducted in silence and interspersed with mass and benediction in the chapel. They were encouraged to read holy books and pamphlets from the library, but on no account to speak to other students. Sean had read the life-story of Matt Talbot and imagined himself wearing chains under his clothes to discipline his body. He enjoyed the long silence of the retreat: it made him feel like a monk.

He was going down the curved 'walk' surrounding the main lawn, when Eddie Doherty came alongside him and tried to talk. He didn't answer or even look sideways at Eddie, but concentrated all his attention on *Stories of the Blessed Sacrament*. It was an interesting book, filled with tales of lights shining around hosts which had been stolen and hidden in the ground and about miraculous movements of chalices in time of danger. Sean was determined that his vow of silence was not going to be broken, but Eddie persisted.

Retribution was very close to them in the person of Byrne, the tall second-prefect. He came from behind, knocked their two heads together and gave each of them a wallop on the ear – one with his right hand and the other with his left. Both blows were equally effective for he was a champion handball player. He walked away from them without a word, leaving Sean to ponder the injustice in new silence.

About a week after the retreat, when all the good resolutions were beginning to fade and life was returning to sinful normality, he heard about the big fight that was to be in the jacks that evening after school. He had already seen a number of fights there between juniors, but this one was special: not only were there seniors involved, but one was a boarder and the other a day-boy. That gave it a special edge.

The school authorities, including the prefects, turned a blind eye to organised fights in the jacks. It was tacitly understood that these were the recognised fair way of settling differences, when other methods had failed: the audience of fellow students was meant to be some sort of guarantee of fair play. He ran to the jacks after the last class of the day and was surprised to find everyone else going in the same direction. He wondered how many others had been sworn to secrecy.

The combatants were already squaring up to each other when Sean pushed his way in to get a good view. Gerry Deehan from Rosemount was the day-boy. His younger brother Jim was in Sean's class: they said he was no 'dozer' when it came to looking after himself. Gerry had the same reputation, but Sean felt sorry for him today, as he compared him with Ben Campbell, the big boarder from South Derry, who looked as if he could crush him with one of his large, red hands. It was town versus country, day-boy against boarder.

Campbell stepped forward and Sean was surprised at the whiteness of his knuckles as he aimed a blow at his lightweight adversary. It was over in a moment and big Campbell lay writhing in pain from a well-directed kick to the groin.

Chapter Fifteen

Sean placed the heel of his hurley on the ground and pressed the shaft a couple of times to test its springiness, just as he had seen his cousin Harry do. The wood had the lovely resilience of good ash. The only blemish was a nick out of the face of it, but that didn't worry Sean at all. Harry had got himself a new, bigger hurley when he had been selected to play on the 'Tech' first team and had given the old one to Sean a week ago, on his fourteenth birthday. He couldn't imagine a better present, particularly as it included a lesson on how to scoop up the ball and strike it, all in one fluid movement.

He placed the hurley on top of the ball and drew it towards him, placing the face of the stick in the path of the rolling ball so that it would run on to it. He lifted the hurley and swung, but made no contact. Next time he snatched too quickly at the rolling ball and it went over the front of the hurley, giving him no chance of a lift. He watched carefully as the next one rolled sweetly on to the wood, lifted at just the right moment and was mindful of Harry's repeated advice to swing 'big and slow'. The ball made a beautiful arc, finishing at the other end of the field. He had never hit a ball so far in his whole life.

He ran to retrieve it at the fence of the Rock field and was surprised to find a bed of nettles there. He trampled them down with his foot and searched with the hurley. It was easier than it used to be when he wore short trousers: you'd never find a lost ball in the nettles in those days without a few stings on the bare legs. There hadn't been nettles there then – he was sure of that. It was here in the soft clay that Sue and he had cleared out little holes to make 'secrets'. She used to call them graves, but he didn't like that name. It was fine to come back in those days and rub away the clay to reveal the glass covering and the flower-petals and silver paper beneath.

He found the ball and ran back, bouncing it on the hurley all the way. He was improving at that, he thought, even though he still needed both hands on the stick. He intended calling into Harry on the way home and he'd let him hear how he was getting on with the *Derry Hornpipe* too. He'd never be as good as Harry on the mouth-organ – he knew that – but he badly wanted to find out how his cousin managed to get the real mouth-organ vamp into the hornpipe. He kept bouncing the ball on the hurley after he had stopped running, turning gradually sideways as he did so, until he was in position for a strike. He gave it all he had and was satisfied to see it landing right in the middle of the Crescent and bouncing past Mackey's front gate.

He had been practising Irish dance music on the mouth-organ every single day since the last Derry Feis. He thought it was a pity that no Protestants ever attended the Feis: they had their own Londonderry festival alright, but they didn't seem to be all that interested in music anyway. As he passed Sue's gate he was shocked to realise that he was thinking of Orla Lynch, whom he had met at the Feis.

Orla was in Jenny's class and had been in the prize-winning choir that afternoon along with her. The result had just been announced and they were all jumping in excitement and hugging one another when Sean went over to congratulate his sister. It was the whiteness of Orla's skin that he noticed and the red flush in her cheeks, but she turned away while he was still trying to think of something to say that would impress her: Jenny told him that Orla would be in the Guildhall again that night.

There was an enormous crowd squeezed up against the black iron gates when he arrived. He panicked at first, thinking he might not get in. On the fifth opening of the gates he was almost lifted in as they surged forward. An attendant tried to tear the correct docket from his season ticket but failed and he found himself in the comparative calm at the bottom of the wide stairway leading up to the main hall.

There was another big crowd outside the hall, but not all of them wanted to get in. They were happy to be chatting and laughing together when they met. As much as anything else, the Feis was a social event, particularly on these last few nights. He could see through the glass doors into the hall, where a lady was singing. He craned sideways and shaded his eyes to read the blackboard: Competition 38, Competitor 9. He skimmed through his programme. It was the soprano competition and that was Cissie Parlour singing.

The doors were opened for a minute when she finished and he pushed in. The attendant changed number nine to number ten on the blackboard and demanded silence for the next competitor. Some of the seated audience showed their displeasure at the noisy entrance of the newcomers. Sean decided to stay where he was and not look for a seat until the next woman had finished. It gave him an opportunity to scan the rows of people.

She wasn't looking at him directly when he spied her over beside the adjudicators' beige-green box, but he was pretty sure she had seen him. He made his way to a seat in the lower balcony so that he could keep an eye on her from the slightly elevated position. When she left her seat later he followed her out to the corridor and managed to bump into her accidentally. He asked her quickly what she thought of the soprano competition, so that she wouldn't escape him. She wanted to know from him what he had really thought of their choir in the afternoon and he realised with pleasure that she was in no hurry to leave. When they separated eventually, to go back into the hall, she said, 'We'll be seeing you, Sean.' He was determined that she would.

He was back in his seat when it struck him that she had used his name. He had called her Orla, of course, but that was different. Throughout the evening he gave each singer and each choir exactly the same number of claps as she did. He felt he was getting to know her. She rose to go after the set dancing and he was at the door before her.

'I'm off,' she said. 'My father gets anxious when I have to go over the bridge late at night.'

He hadn't expected it to be so easy.

'Can I leave you home?' he asked.

'That's very kind of you,' she said.

Somehow, he hadn't thought of it like that, but it made him feel good.

The feeling lasted until they were half-way over the bridge: from then on, he was uncomfortably aware of the fact that he was leaving a girl home for the first time and didn't know what was expected of him at the end of the journey. They had already been through his music and her music, his class and her class, his friends and her friends, his teachers and her teachers: it didn't leave a lot more to say, but she had the last word about twenty yards from her own house.

'Good night,' she shouted, as she ran for the gate, 'safe home.'

It was over and he had done it – no problem at all. He turned back towards the Guildhall and home, with a light step.

The memory of the Feis had begun to fade and the big thing in his life was handball. He could neither think nor talk about anything else. It had started when he had got the American handball with the elephant embossed on it. It was a bribe from Larry Doak, to ensure Sean's help with maths. Larry's uncle worked for the Yanks and seemed to be able to procure anything his nephew wanted.

The little ball bounced high above Sean's head and he ran back to strike it. It was sorer on the hands than a tennis ball, which was what they normally used on the alley, and it bounced twice as high. It would take some getting used to, but he'd be a real handball player by that time.

'Fr Ruane wants to see you up in his room,' a boarder shouted to him from the tennis court.

He had been expecting the call for some time now. Nearly everyone in his class had been up for their little chat about life. He hoped the priest wouldn't ask him what he intended to do when he left school. It would be hard to explain why he was no longer going on for the Church: yet he was studying Greek. He knew a priest couldn't be committing the sort of private sins he was involved with, but he certainly wouldn't like to try and explain that to Fr Ruane. It was bad enough in the darkness of the confessional with a strange priest!

But there was no mention of anything like that. Fr Ruane started to ask about handball. Sean knew he must have seen him practising from the window of his room in the Junior House. Why couldn't he leave him in peace? After handball it was football and they discussed the College league, in which Sea had no great interest. He knew from the other fellows in his class that this was the way the conversation always went. When the priest cleared his throat with a nervous little cough they both knew that it was the moment of truth.

'Well, Sean,' he said, 'I didn't bring you up here to talk about football.'

'No, Father.' The smoke from the cigarette was getting into his eyes. It always did.

'I wanted to talk to you about your body.'

'Yes, Father.' His eyes were streaming. Fr Ruane had given him the cigarette to put him at his ease. Some ease, he thought, as he screwed up his eyes in pain.

Then it was procreation and the holy sacrament of marriage No matter how he held the cigarette, the wisping smoke found a direct path to his eyes. It disturbed his concentration on holy purity and the production of seed.

It wasn't really a conversation. All that was required of Sean was an affirmation or a denial at the right time and Fr Ruane would then continue his uncomfortable story. They had reached wet dreams when Sean gave an answer that indirectly revealed the awful truth that he had never experienced this delight. The priest started to back-pedal towards holy purity and the safety of the Church's general teaching, wondering what damage he had done.

Sean knew it was time to go when they reached handball

again. Fr Ruane didn't try to keep him any longer, but wished
him well with the handball and said he'd see him again next year
for a chat. He was glad to get home and leave the College
behind him.

One little corner of Hatrick's field, away out the Buncrana
Road, was blue again with mayflower. It was the same every
year: the whole family would come out to gather wild flowers
for the May altar, climbing over the fence to rediscover the
quivering blue that no-one else seemed to know.

They used to have only one altar in the kitchen: it was nothing more than a statue of the Blessed Virgin with a vase in front
of it. Then Sean decided to have an altar of his own in the bedroom: the girls, feeling they had to be 'upsides' with him, now
had one in their room, but without the candles and missal-stand
that he had. Those were relics of the days he used to play at
being a priest. That was long ago, he thought.

Mary was collecting daisies and Eamonn already had difficulty in containing all his buttercups in one hand: they dropped
in a bright line of yellow behind him as he moved.

'Come here till we see if you like butter,' he shouted to
Mary and held the buttercup beneath her chin. 'Yes, it says you
like it alright,' he said, stooping to look at the yellow reflection
under her chin.

'Let me try it on you,' she asked, but he was already running
over to Sean.

'That's stupid, Eamonn,' said his big brother. 'Sure everybody knows rightly I like butter.'

'Aye, but the buttercup is a sure test for anybody at all, if you can see the yellow shining under their chin.'

Jenny came over to them. 'Here, Mary,' she said, 'see if I like it.'

'Well?' Jenny asked expectantly.

'I can't see it,' Mary cried. 'Is it yellow, Sean?'

He walked away from them, already tired of picking the flowers and wondering why he had come. How could he have thought it so marvellous before?

Eamonn shouted after him, 'Jenny does like butter and it's not stupid at all. You're the one that's stupid.'

Sean climbed over the low wall and sat down in the dusty grass at the side of the road to wait for them. He could see people getting on the Buncrana bus, far along the road on his right. He watched the bus as it accelerated towards him and wished he was on it now, speeding well away from this place.

At least it's nearly summer, he thought, and it won't be long till we go swimming again at Fahan. That had always been a long, long run on the bike and you'd really feel the joy of a dip after the ten hot, dusty miles.

'Come on: we're goin' home,' said Brid. 'We have plenty of flowers.'

She lifted Mary over the wall and turned for Eamonn, but he pushed her away and climbed shakily over by himself. Brid took the weans, one in each hand, and the three of them started homewards.

'I'm goin' to Fahan,' Sean shouted after her. He was surprised to hear the words himself. That wasn't really what he had wanted to say.

'Don't be silly,' Brid said over her shoulder. 'We're goin' home now, for Mammy'll have the dinner ready.'

'Well, I'm not goin' and that's all about it. I'm for walkin' to Fahan.' He was sure of himself now.

'You're not serious, Sean – are you?' Jenny half-whispered to him from the other side of the wall.

'Of course I am: are you comin'?'

'Why not?' she laughed. 'At least I'll give it a try.' She sat up on the wall, swung her legs over and jumped down on the road. 'Come on if you're comin' then,' she said.

He looked along the road and saw Brid hurrying the reluctant weans home. She shook Mary's arm angrily when the child turned round to see where himself and Jenny were going. He waved to Mary and turned to follow Jenny.

It was two miles to the Customs Station at Bridgend. He was surprised that none of the men with the peaked caps stopped them: they could have been smuggling anything. Another couple of miles brought them to Burnfoot and a small shop full of groceries and sweets. They looked in the window at brandyballs in a big jar and bars of sticky toffee. He could almost feel how nice it would be to break off each square of it with a snap. But he had no money in his pocket, so he turned away. He thought of the dinner at home: the others would have finished it long since. It was better not to think about it, but just keep on walking.

Hours later, Jenny was sure they were lost, but he assured her they were nearly there, trying to sound as if he really knew. His feet and ankles throbbed but he continued to urge Jenny not to lag behind him. Then, when he least expected it, the bright strand of Fahan appeared through a gap in the hedge and the long pier stood out into the calm waters of Lough Swilly.

'We're there, Jenny: we're there. Come here till you see.'

She quickened her pace to catch up with him. 'Oh, it's gorgeous, isn't it, Sean? I don't feel tired at all now.'

They ran down to the strand: it seemed to him far bigger than ever before, with the tide away out. They raced to the pier along the smooth, damp sand.

Across Lough Swilly he could see the tiny pier of Rathmullan on the other side. It always reminded him of Sue: her family used to go on holidays there, taking the ferry across from Fahan. How often had he stood on this pier, looking across in the hope of catching the slightest glimpse of her. He felt an emptiness inside him.

They took off their shoes and socks and paddled in the freezing water.

'That's lovely,' said Jenny, 'I'm beginning to get the feeling back into my poor feet again.'

It was only when they were drying their feet with their stockings that he realised that another ten tiring miles of road separated them from Derry. It was already teatime – his stomach told him that: the intermittent hunger pangs had now become a constant ache.

'If we were home now we'd be havin' bread and jam,' said Jenny. 'I'd love that.'

'Don't be thinkin' about it,' said Sean. 'Come on now: let's strike out fast for Derry. It's far worse when you go slow.'

He was still conscious of the wonder of having walked all the way – he had the beating of the bus and train now, even if it had taken him a while longer. Anybody could do it on a bike. Somehow he didn't credit Jenny with his achievement, since she had only followed him: he had to admit, though, that she had great heart.

'Do you think we'll ever get home, Sean?' Her voice quivered ever so slightly.

'Of course we will,' he said firmly. 'It must be over two hours since we left Fahan, so we're not far off Burnfoot now.' The sun had gone in and a cool evening breeze blew. He knew from the dullness that it was getting late. Two cows with big swinging udders were being driven towards them by a young fellow of his own age. He could hear the rattle of buckets in the byre as the woman of the house prepared for milking.

'Hi there,' the young drover shouted to him. 'Kep them cattle.'

Sean waved his arms in front of them and they turned reluctantly into the farmyard.

'Hup,' shouted the lad, as he gave one of them a swish of the branch he carried.

Sean stayed watching as the cows ambled slowly into the byre. He heard the noise of the chains as they were tied in their stalls. He strained to hear the comforting sound of milk squirting into a bucket and saw the boy washing his hands under a tap at the door of the byre: he cupped them and made loud suckings as he drank. He straightened himself and shook the water from his hands, dried his mouth with his shirtsleeve and walked towards the house. He nodded as he went in. The rattle of knives and forks and the clinking of cups was their signal to turn away and continue their unending pilgrimage to Derry.

Burnfoot was behind them at last and Bridgend too: he even thought he could see the spire of Pennyburn in the distance.

'I have to sit down, Sean.' Jenny's weary voice came from

behind him. 'I can't go any further.'

'Just keep goin' as far as Hatrick's field and we'll have a nice rest there.' He knew he'd have to coax her, so he went back to where she was stopped. 'Just don't think about it and your feet'll take you there.'

A woman carrying a basket and accompanied by three children came towards them, silhouetted against the evening sky. The eldest was a girl and she held the hand of the youngest, another girl. The boy was running towards them, waving wildly.

'It's Mammy and the rest of them,' Sean said in surprise.

'God, so it is,' said Jenny. 'She's goin' to kill us.'

'I bet you she won't,' Sean said confidently. He could see the big red flask sticking out of his mother's basket and he knew there'd be sandwiches as well.

'Did you do it?' Eamonn asked. 'Did you reach Fahan?'

'Aye,' said Sean, 'there and back.'

'They walked to Fahan – all the way,' Eamonn shouted back to his mother.

She had already put down her basket and was opening the flask. 'Have a hot drink of tea,' she said. 'We thought you were lost.'

Jenny took the cup in her two hands and sat in the ditch: he saw the tears welling in her eyes.

'What are you cryin' for now?' Sean asked her. 'Sure didn't we do it?' He felt her happy tears inside himself, but he wouldn't show them.

His mother fussed around them with more sandwiches and Brid had a bag of freshly-made queen cakes. The weans wanted to know what exactly himself and Jenny had been doing and whether they'd had a dip or not. Brid told them to be quiet until the picnic was over. His mother had brought a damp facecloth and a towel, so that they could freshen themselves up. Brid handed him the cloth and his mother held the towel until he was ready for it.

'You'll feel the better of that,' she said. He was glad to know again the feeling of belonging.

Clouds were gathering behind them, far out towards Inishowen. He turned away and saw the winking lights of Derry in the distance. He wanted to go home.